"Leo?"

A whisper was all Amy could manage as she stared in shaky disbelief up at the tall man, cataloging every detail of his patrician features, every shift of expression on his face, all angles and intriguing hollows strong classic features. A miracle of symmetry acted like a trip switch that turned her brain off as she experienced a weird collision of past and present.

Seeing him that last time, the hurt and disillusion on his face before he walked away. There was no hurt now. His dark eyes were shuttered, stance relaxed, though there was a telltale tension in his flexing jawline that some might miss. But she knew that face, or at least a younger version of it so well, she didn't miss anything. Not the tiny scar by the side of his mouth—she remembered tracing it with her finger—or the waves of sinful male magnetism that poured off him.

Kim Lawrence lives on a farm in Anglesey with her university-lecturer husband, assorted pets who arrived as strays and never left, and sometimes one or both of her boomerang sons. When she's not writing, she loves to be outdoors gardening or walking on one of the beaches for which the island is famous—along with being the place where Prince William and Catherine made their first home!

Books by Kim Lawrence

Harlequin Presents

Claimed by Her Greek Boss
Awakened in Her Enemy's Palazzo
His Wedding Day Revenge
Engaged in Deception
Last-Minute Vows

Jet-Set Billionaires

Innocent in the Sicilian's Palazzo

The Secret Twin Sisters

The Prince's Forbidden Cinderella
Her Forbidden Awakening in Greece

Visit the Author Profile page
at Harlequin.com for more titles.

RECLAIMED ON ROMANO'S TERMS

KIM LAWRENCE

PRESENTS

MIX
Paper | Supporting responsible forestry
FSC
www.fsc.org
FSC® C021394

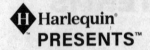

Harlequin®
PRESENTS™

Recycling programs for this product may not exist in your area.

ISBN-13: 978-1-335-21348-8

Reclaimed on Romano's Terms

Harlequin Enterprises ULC
22 Adelaide St. West, 41st Floor
Toronto, Ontario M5H 4E3, Canada
www.Harlequin.com

HarperCollins Publishers
Macken House, 39/40 Mayor Street Upper,
Dublin 1, D01 C9W8, Ireland
www.HarperCollins.com

Printed in Lithuania

RECLAIMED ON ROMANO'S TERMS

For Stella.

PROLOGUE

THE LIGHTS THAT had been on earlier when they left the house were still blazing as the car turned into the long tree-lined driveway of the Manor. In the driver's seat Amy's father was silent, as he had been the entire journey back from the hospital.

It wasn't a relaxed, comfortable silence; it was a tense, nerve-stretching absence of sound. The only times he had even acknowledged her presence was when he'd delivered a series of poisonous icy glares when she had dared risk a surreptitious glance at the numerous missed messages on her phone screen.

Amy's fingers remained curled around the phone but after a swift sideways glance at her father's profile— even his double chin looked furious—she didn't pull it out. A spasm of self-contempt tugged the corners of her lips downward.

Not so brave now, sneered the voice in her head.

Earlier, it had been a different story.

She had stood defiant in the face of her parents' reaction, even though normally her mother would act as the voice of moderation whenever she incurred her father's displeasure, but not this time.

Her parents had been united in their horror.

Amy shook her head as though the action would physically block the scene that continued to play out in her head in a loop.

It didn't.

'How far has this gone?' her father thundered inside her head as the replay loop reached the cliffhanger moment.

'How far has it gone…?' she'd repeated. 'No further than I wanted it to.'

Her mother whimpered and gasped, '*My baby!*'

The memory of that response twisted the knife of guilt a few painful inches deeper in Amy's chest.

'Mum, this isn't a Victorian melodrama and I'm not a child. I'm nineteen next week.'

Lost in her own miserable thoughts, she didn't notice the engine had been switched off until her father opened the car door, still ignoring her. Amy caught his sleeve and he swung around, his eyes sliding from her face to her hand grasping the tweed of his jacket.

When she let go, he smoothed the fabric as though she had contaminated it with her touch.

'Mum will be all right, won't she, Dad?'

Despite the doctors' confident assertions, Amy still found it difficult to believe, even after her prayers had been answered and her mother had regained consciousness.

Amy would have promised anything at that moment, and she had.

She flinched now as her father's response was a slammed door.

The security lights came on as he marched towards the front door they must have left wide open in their hurry to leave in the slipstream of the ambulance's blue flashing lights.

Biting her already raw full lower lip, Amy extricated herself from the passenger seat and stood in the shadows of the semi lit forecourt. The night air hit her, cooling her skin but not the swirling mass of tormented emotions twisting in her head.

Out of habit, she glanced up at the clock tower above the arch that led to the stable block, her eyes widening when she saw it was one-thirty. Had it *really* only been six hours earlier when she had stood, bag packed, telling her parents of her intention to leave? She knew her over-confident declaration had been defensively aggressive to compensate for the fact her knees were shaking and her stomach churning in apprehension.

Having spent her life wrapped in cotton wool that had come to feel like a strait jacket she was breaking free of, taking a massive step into the unknown and facing parental disapproval, it was small wonder her knees had been shaking.

Six hours—which meant that Leo had been waiting for her for five hours by now. She had allowed herself a comfortable hour to get to their prearranged meeting spot. She had been terrified of being late and somehow missing him.

Was he still waiting?

What had he thought when she didn't show?

Amy's cold fingers tightened around the phone in her pocket. She wished she could regain some of her earlier bravery, that utter certainty of several hours ago that had buoyed her.

That certainty had dissolved as she'd witnessed her

mother's body jerk like a broken doll in response to the shock from the paddles the paramedics had administered. The horror she'd felt had killed all her confidence stone dead, even before her father had snarled, *'You did this!'*

Amy was no longer made brave by the naive conviction that love would make everything all right. The conviction that had made her stand quietly throughout a storm of accusations and threats, culminating in her father's parting shot.

'Walk through that door and that's it—I have no daughter.'

The ultimatum had shaken her but she'd held her ground. 'You won't accept that I'm with Leo, but I love him and I know we're meant to be together. I have no choice.'

She knew differently now; there *was* a choice and it was one she had made when her mother had regained consciousness and pulled off her oxygen mask long enough to plead.

'Don't do this, Amy, don't go with him—promise me, promise me.'

'I promise, Mum.'

Amy walked towards the open door, but her father had already disappeared from view. The elegant chandelier illuminated the graceful curving staircase that Amy had been halfway down when her mother's anguished cry had made Amy turn in time to see her clutch her chest and collapse.

She had a vague recollection of running back up the stairs and falling on her knees by her mother's prone form.

Her father had been there too, his face as red as her mother's had been pale. 'Are you happy now that you've nearly killed her?'

Amy blinked back tears as the scene continued to relentlessly play out in her head. She stared at the phone in her hand, remembering how she'd had to yell to make herself heard above her father's abusive flow of bitter accusations as she gave the requested details to the emergency services.

'Is she breathing?' she'd been asked.

'I don't know!' Amy had wailed, frustration and gut-clenching fear making it hard to respond to the calm instructions of the person on the other end of the line.

'Yes, I think her airway is clear…but her lips are blue. Chest compressions? I… Right…'

When the paramedic had appeared, she had literally sobbed her relief, the floodgates opening and tears falling in a river down her cheeks as she fell back onto her heels and manoeuvred herself out of their way.

The journey behind the ambulance remained a surreal blur. The arrival in the casualty unit was equally dream-like, but certain details stood out, like seeing the heart emoji on her phone screen when they had been asked to switch off mobiles as they walked through what felt like a sinister forest of bleeping machines to the cubicle where her mum lay, surrounded by a scary number of medical staff.

As she reached the first of the flight of steps that led to the front door, Amy heard footsteps from inside the house and braced her shoulders, fighting an urge to delay the moment when she would be alone with her father.

She was working up her courage when a rustle made her turn her head in time to see a tall, lean figure separate itself from the purple-shadowed glossy undergrowth.

'Leo!' Shock and longing were intertwined in her gasp as she identified the figure standing there. 'I… I… *You* can't be here.' She looked nervously over her shoulder. The situation was awful enough without Leo, who didn't have a clue what it was like to be on the receiving end of her father's temper.

He took a step forward, the light illuminating his features. It highlighted the sharp cheekbones, the symmetrical planes and hollows, his perfect features dissected by a narrow blade of a nose, the sculpted sultry curve of his incredible mouth.

The shadows did nothing to dilute his masculine aura, the tingling charge of danger he gave off. The danger had initially attracted her, but it was his passion and sensitivity that had kept her with him, that had turned her lust to love.

The high-octane masculinity hit her now like a shockwave, grabbing hard at the muscles low in her belly, the longing so strong she could barely breathe. The sense of loss that followed felt like a hard, dark weight lodged behind her breastbone.

'Where have you been, Amy?' He moved closer and the light hit his face, leaving half in darkness, half in light. The emotions in his dark eyes reached out to grab her. He wasn't angry, just frustrated and confused, his dark brows drawn into a questioning line above his hawkish nose as he stared at her. 'I waited for you…'

She knew it was crazy but it was a fact; she could *feel*

his voice. Deep velvet with a fascinating back note of gravel, it vibrated through every cell in her body.

'What have they done to you?'

She stood there on the balls of her feet, poised to run into the arms he held open in invitation. An invitation she longed to accept, to walk into his arms to feel the hardness of his lean body, smell the warm male scent of his skin. The longing rose up in her and she wanted nothing more than to lay her head against his chest and hear his heartbeat and feel his strong arms close protectively around her.

She wanted the rest of the world to go away and there to be nothing but her and Leo.

When Leo was with her she felt braver and stronger; it always felt as if he'd peeled away a layer and exposed the real her. With him, she was more *herself* than she had ever been before she'd met him. The same way his lovemaking seemed to somehow drive her deeper into herself, making her self-aware at a cellular level in a way she could not define.

'Is sex always like this?' she had asked him after that first time, because she'd had nothing to compare it to.

'Not for me it isn't,' he'd replied, looking as stunned as she had felt.

Her eyes on his face like a sleepwalker, she took a half step towards him, remembering as she did so how she'd felt the first time she'd set eyes on him. Her nervous system had gone into meltdown, her brain short-circuited. She had never experienced anything so *visceral* in her life before.

He had terrified her, not because there was anything threatening in his behaviour; despite his physicality, the opposite was true. The way his big hands with their long, tapering brown fingers had moved down the nervous colt's flanks was incredibly gentle.

She had been too stunned in the moment by the whirlwind of sensation inside her to register how the skittish animal responded to the soft words the most beautiful man she had ever imagined was murmuring into its ear. Sensing her presence, he had turned his head, brushing his hands along the torn denim that covered his muscular thighs.

Amy had shivered as fire crackled along her nerve-endings when his dark eyes connected with her stare. She could see the flare of awareness flash in his, and then he'd smiled and she was lost.

'I am so sorry, Leo,' she pushed out, feeling the heat of tears that pressed against her eyelids. The deep ache of loss in her belly.

From nowhere, the rain came. Under the shelter of the porticoed porch she stayed dry, but in seconds Leo was drenched—not that he reacted to it, or the water that ran down his face, glossing his golden skin—skin she loved to touch.

In her peripheral vision she was aware of her father appearing in the doorway behind her. She half turned and saw that he was holding a phone in his hand, wielding it like a weapon, not looking at her but at Leo.

'I've already called the police to tell them we have an intruder. I'm filming this, so keep your distance!' he added, even though Leo hadn't moved. But without moving at all he suddenly seemed taller and even more imposing.

Leo stared her father down before his glance shifted

to Amy, lingering on her face for a long moment. There was no doubt in his face, just encouragement. The fact he believed in her and had total confidence that she would take the hand he stretched towards her made not doing so the most painful thing she'd ever experienced in her life.

Amy saw the brief look of confusion flicker across his chiselled features before he switched his scrutiny to her father.

'I didn't come here to argue with you. I just came here for Amy.'

Amy stared again at the hand extended to her, the internal conflict that was raging inside her finding release in a series of white-faced, agonised gasps. 'You don't understand, Leo.'

For three seconds their eyes held, then he broke the contact as his hand fell down. 'I think maybe I do. You want this.' His hand lifted again but this time his sweeping gesture encompassed the illuminated manor house. 'You like your designer life, you love it…the tennis clubs, the skiing holidays. You were never going to walk away from it all, were you?' His shoulders lifted in a shrug as one dark brow elevated. 'I get it,' he ground out, his gorgeous voice now sounding like broken glass.

'No, it's not like that at all! I just can't…'

'Amy.'

Her father's voice stopped her in her tracks.

'I am so sorry, Leo, but—'

His head reared back as he made a cutting gesture with his hand. 'I don't need buts. Goodbye, Amy. It's certainly been an…experience.'

He turned and walked away, taking something of Amy with him.

CHAPTER ONE

Nine years later

LEO ROMANO, WHO WAS walking and talking as he spoke into his phone, paused by the glass wall that afforded thrilling views across the City landscape. But he ignored the view as he ended the call with a crisp, *'Ciao.'*

He slid the phone into a pocket of the tailored dark jeans he wore and applied the towel hanging loosely around his neck to his wet hair before discarding it in a crumpled heap. It landed wetly on one of the designer leather chairs arranged to enjoy the view as he shook his head, leaving speckles of moisture on the dark blue of the silk shirt that he had not yet buttoned. It hung open, revealing a slice of his golden, densely muscled torso. His broad chest had a light dusting of dark body hair, his flat belly was ridged with muscle. The dull gold buckle of his unfastened belt was a shade lighter than his skin.

Fastening his shirt one-handed, he paused by the open laptop set on a table. The screen was frozen on a shot of a slim figure. In the background, the building she was leaving was totally blocked out by hordes of press wielding sound booms, microphones and cameras. There was no sound on the clip but it had to be bedlam, yet she appeared calm, if very pale, with her eyes fixed on a point up ahead, her tilted chin displaying the graceful curve of her neck.

The rich caramel-coloured hair—hair he had once tangled his fingers in—was drawn back from her face in a thick glossy braid that was pinned around her oval face. The puritanical hairstyle left nothing to hide behind, but there was nothing to hide.

Amy Sinclair was beautiful, more so now than she had been nine years ago.

The delicate bone structure of her face and melting softness of her wide-spaced, darkly-lashed brown eyes were perfectly balanced by feathery dark brows and the lush curve of her mouth—a mouth that had launched a thousand fantasies. Many of those fantasies, he thought grimly, belonged to him.

Leo looked away, resenting the degree of effort it took to break the connection, unable to deny the scalding rush of frustrated heat that had settled in his groin. It was humiliating for a man who prided himself on his total objectivity, the ability to take the emotion out of decision-making or, for that matter, from life in general. Amy's rejection had made him the man he was today, so he had that much to thank her for.

Taking a couple of deep breaths, lips compressed, hands clenched tight with his long brown fingers bone-white from the pressure, he forced himself to turn back. It would have been simpler to pretend he felt nothing, but after nine years the act was wearing thin.

The moment had come to break the cycle of denial, face his weakness and conquer it.

Some might say not before time, he thought, his nostrils flaring as he huffed out a snort of impatient self-contempt.

For nine years he had told himself that the Sinclair family were history, consigned to some dusty corner of his mind.

He had moved on.

It was a self-delusion that had been exposed the moment the George Sinclair scandal had spawned a wealth of banner headlines: Wealthy Financier Caught with Hand in the Till.

It would have been reasonable, given their shared history, to indulge in a few moments of what-goes-around-comes-around satisfaction, raise a glass to karma then get on with his life.

Instead, he had become totally…*obsessed* with the story. Even admitting to this weakness in the privacy of his own head, just *thinking* the word made him clench his teeth, but what else could you call his encyclopaedic knowledge of every tabloid headline, every online podcast covering Sinclair's trial and eventual incarceration? He'd also hoarded every scrap of information, including every photo, old or new, of Sinclair's daughter, whose *loyalty* and *quiet dignity* had apparently won her a fan base.

There were a lot of photos and he had looked at every single one of them.

Leo had read it all and filed away the opinions of both the crazy people and the serious commentators. Those who loved Amy Sinclair for being a dutiful, loving daughter were countered by an equal number of conspiracy theorists who had concluded she was the criminal mastermind behind the crime and she'd got off scot-free, while the real crazies framed a possibility that she came from Mars.

He had read it all, watched it all—and all because nine years ago Amy Sinclair had rejected him.

Something he had recovered from completely.

Having the lie revealed for what it was meant he was not well-disposed towards the author of his humiliation or, more especially, himself.

It wasn't as if he was the only person in the world to be rejected by his first love, and it wasn't as if rejection had been a new experience for him. Sure, his mother hadn't exactly *rejected* him, but she had died, which as a child had felt pretty much like the same thing.

Then came the foster homes, where a couple of unpleasant experiences had left their mark, but most carers had been well-intentioned, or even kind, but by that point in his life Leo had been wary of *kind*. Even the better people he'd come across had found the aloof kid he'd been too self-contained. A child who didn't smile or cry was hard to warm to.

School hadn't supplied the sort of stimulation his quick mind had craved. His last report had basically read: *a bit of a loner, but good with animal*s. When he'd met Amy Sinclair, he'd been working at stables that ran a sanctuary sideline for old and abused horses. She had been one of the rich kid volunteers, the sort he'd normally steered clear of.

Amy was the first person in his life who had believed in him. Except, of course, she hadn't. She'd simply strung him along as they had created a future together in their heads, but when push came to shove, the novelty value of slumming it had inevitably worn off. And when faced with the prospect of actually leaving her spoilt, fairy tale princess lifestyle for a life with a *no-hope loser* as her father had so charmingly phrased it, she had revealed her true self.

Leo didn't look back on the immediate post-Amy era of his life with any pride, those weeks and months when he had wallowed in self-pity, often found in the bottom of a glass. But he had eventually come out the other side and moved on, telling himself, and really believing it, that he had shrugged off the past and learnt from it. He had viewed, and still did, the gullibility of his old self with a mixture of embarrassment, scorn and disbelief.

And there were even positives to the experience, which he had acknowledged; he had definitely learnt some very important lessons.

He'd never thought of a woman as *his* again, and never would. The term *soulmate* had been expunged from his vocabulary. Somewhere between the bottom of a beer glass and deciding to fight back, Leo had discovered that being a lone wolf and thinking outside the box did not make you a loser.

Actually, those traits could be positive ones when it came to making money, as his early success in crypto had shown. The self-belief that success had given him had helped him deal in a pragmatic way with the next bolt from the blue when it came.

He had family in the form of an Italian billionaire grandfather, who appeared to think that Leo would view this news like a lottery winner and run after the dangling carrot he'd extended. Whereas, actually, Leo's first inclination had been to tell this stranger, who had turfed out his only daughter because she had fallen in love with a man he didn't approve of, to take a hike. Leo had no interest in being the chosen one, and he was more than capable of making his own success; he didn't need to inherit it.

'You think I care about the Romano name, or how old and *noble* this family is, or how much money you have? *You* came looking for *me* because there isn't anyone else, but maybe you should have thought of that before you threw my mother out. I'm not about to kiss your ring or anywhere else, old man, because you need me more than I need you!'

A faint, ironic smile tugged at Leo's lips at the memory of that first encounter, which had been, to put it politely, *stormy*. Over the years, there had been several storms while he worked alongside his grandfather, and even now that the old man was no longer taking an active part in the day-to-day working of the Romano estate, there were still occasions when they butted heads.

Men who threw their daughters to the wolves did not fill Leo with admiration, but over the years an understanding of sorts had developed between the two men.

His heavy-lidded glance strayed one last time to the screen.

He wasn't filled with admiration for weak, compliant daughters who supported their guilty fathers, either.

His half-smile had vanished, and his eyes were cold as he closed the laptop with a decisive snap. He had allowed ghosts from the past to take up space in his head. Now, he needed to free up that space and reclaim his life, which, as lives went, was a pretty good one.

Nine years ago, he had not been in a position to take revenge on the family responsible for humiliating him.

Flexing his broad shoulders, he reached for the leather jacket he had discarded earlier. He was the one calling the shots now.

As he slid into the driving seat of his car, he glanced at the time on the slim platinum-banded watch on his wrist. It was a thirty-minute drive to where the fast-food truck where Amy produced culinary miracles, according to the reviews he'd read, was parked up.

She had gone from being the head chef at a fashionable Michelin-starred restaurant in the capital owned by her father to running a fast-food truck. Her fall in social and professional standing had been as meteoric as his journey in the opposite direction had been.

According to his research, she would still be there. Apparently, she always put in a long day and her only help was a kid on a government employment scheme and a well-known chef who had fallen off the wagon and on hard times.

Amy *should* have fallen apart without *Daddy* to tell her what to do, *Daddy* to buy her a restaurant as a plaything, *Daddy* who, for all he knew, still had to approve her boyfriends.

Yes, Leo had confidently waited for her to fall apart. But she hadn't.

It was common knowledge that she had received multiple offers from tabloids to tell her story, casting herself in a favourable light. But it turned out she had not taken up even one of the book offers that would have established her as a professional victim, with her story eventually serialised profitably in one of the red-tops.

Leo assumed she had money stashed away and was

biding her time to push the price up, a risky strategy. But there hadn't been a bidding war, no sob story; instead, she'd resurfaced as the part owner of Gourmet Gypsy, a glorified greasy spoon food truck—not anyone's idea of an easy route.

Despite being a social pariah, she obviously still had a few friends in the industry, because some low-key publicity for her down-market venture had emerged. A couple of food critics had written good things, and she was making a living of sorts.

She was called resilient; she was called imaginative and hard-working.

It took a tough person to do what Amy had, but Leo knew she was *not* tough. Reading praise, however faint, of her was like hearing a nail scratching a chalkboard.

Then when her father had been released from incarceration early and the information filtered through to Leo about the sudden increase in Sinclair's cash-flow, he finally understood what was going on. Amy always had followed Daddy's orders and this was all part of her father's long-term plan. Her business was just a front for him to help out his new friends with a bit of money laundering.

Could she really be part of this latest con, or was she just a dim, unwitting pawn? It was time to find out.

Half an hour later, Leo had parked up.

His position, giving him a view of the SilverStream with *Gourmet Gypsy* written along its sides, was pretty much perfect. The interior was still illuminated and he could make out a figure moving around inside.

Then the lights went out, the door opened, and he

watched as a small figure, slim beneath an unattractive padded coat that reached to mid-thigh, pulled down the shutters and locked up.

She seemed unaware of a group of three or four youths in hoodies sharing a bottle they passed between them, their lurching progress suggesting they were not just high on booze.

Like many parts of London, extreme deprivation sat cheek by jowl with wealth and privilege. The Gourmet Gypsy van sat squarely on the dividing line between the boarded-up windows and the chic, expensive shops, in a sort of no-man's-land.

Leo got out of the car and, as he did so, the irony hit him. He had come to punish her and instead he might actually end up saving her.

CHAPTER TWO

AMY WAS DOG-TIRED, although she almost welcomed the exhaustion as it stopped her worrying. She worried a lot, but lately, since she had agreed to her father's suggestion that she put her name to his new venture, she worried even more.

She was, of course, glad that he had regained some focus and proud that he wanted to rebuild his life and repay the investors who had lost out because of what he called his *bad decisions*. He'd complained that there were unfair obstacles stopping someone like him rebuilding their life, making a success of himself.

It had been a relief to see the fire in his eyes when he had come up with a way to overcome those obstacles. Since he had been released early from prison, he had accused her of watching him like a hawk and, although she denied it, she was.

Amy would never forget that terrible night after he had been given bail before the trial, when she'd found him lying on the sofa surrounded by empty pill bottles. She hadn't been watching him then—she'd been so angry with him she'd spent as little time in his company as possible, and he had almost died.

'But I don't understand—what are they investing in?'

There was no way her business was worth a fraction of the sort of sums she had glimpsed on the documents her father had wanted her to sign.

She had been wary, but was terrified of how he might react if she didn't show she had faith in him. Though, in all honesty, she couldn't see the business justifying the investment and the suppliers she already had were cheaper than the contracts her father was so proud of negotiating. She was already working twenty-four-seven to keep her head above water, to make a go of Gourmet Gypsy without the additional overheads, and what sort of influence would these investors want for their money?

But she'd wanted to make her father happy. He was, after all, the only family she had left after her mother had died just before he was arrested.

He had assured her that the investors would not interfere. All he needed was her signature—a lot of signatures, it seemed to Amy, and when she had wanted to read the papers she was putting her name to, her father had looked hurt and asked her if she didn't trust him.

He had served his time and paid a heavy price for his crime, he'd declared. He deserved a second chance, and if his own daughter wouldn't give him one, who would?

Amy fished out her phone from her pocket and glanced at the clock, estimating what time she'd arrive home. Despite her father being pretty sniffy about the flat, she couldn't really afford it. But she'd needed a second bedroom for him when he was released, and she liked it. The top floor afforded views of trees and while the brick, purpose-built block wasn't pretty, it was quiet Also, it was only five minutes from the Tube, so all she had was a ten-minute walk the other end.

She hadn't put the phone back in her deep pocket before it was snatched out of her hand. Amy jolted back to the moment with a thud by the adrenaline dump into her bloodstream, and she took in the boys, faces invisible, that she had been oblivious to. Boys now circling her...laughing, jeering. She let out a sharp cry of protest and ignored the voice in her head that suggested she should run.

She couldn't afford a new phone and her whole life was on it.

'It's a really old phone—you don't need it, I do.' She tried to inject calm reason into her voice but could barely hear her words, let alone the intonation, above the thud of her own heartbeat vibrating in her eardrums.

'Need it!' mocked the one holding her phone. '*Posh*, isn't she...?' He turned with a flood of expletives and a titter and found his companions were not where they'd just been. He couldn't think why they had run and the phone he had just been tauntingly holding up had been snatched back. 'Bitch!' he snarled and grabbed her.

Amy had sometimes imagined how she would react in a situation of this sort, never actually thinking it would happen. Because it didn't, did it? Things like this happened to someone else. She had always decided that a brains rather than brawn response would be the best plan, given she was only five foot three. Her first option was to run, and she was actually quite fast, but if that wasn't an option she would try talking her way out of the situation.

Resorting to violence had never been one of the options.

It turned out that reality differed from theory big time! Blind instinct along with panic kicked in and she began

to struggle wildly as she wriggled, feeling a small moment of satisfaction as she stepped down hard on something she thought—she hoped—was a foot.

The grunt and curse suggested it was. But then the
arm around her neck tightened and ice-cold brain-
numbing fear conquered every other emotion.

She felt darkness lower across her vision and nerve-
less fingers dropped the phone—but then, quite suddenly, she could breathe again. As her brain sparked into
life she was aware, in her peripheral vision, of someone
who was very tall. Like a puppet whose strings had been
severed she fell to her knees and stayed there, breathing
hard. Aware too that things were happening off-camera
while she fought the urge to vomit.

She eventually got to her feet and, with her eyes still
squished closed, addressed her hoarse question to a point
over her shoulder. 'Have they gone?'

'They have gone.' A few harsh words followed in a
language she could identify but didn't know.

The voice she could identify in any language.

Amy didn't need to look. She knew that voice at a cellular level, as well as the person it belonged to.

She had no clue in the world how he was here, but
he was.

Had she gone mad?

Or sustained a knock on the head?

Both seemed a lot more likely than Leo being here in
this place, now. Her heart hammering against her ribcage, she lifted her braced hands off her thighs, her palms
slick with sweat. She straightened up slowly and, with
one hand anchoring her messed hair that had come adrift
during the short, frantic tussle, she opened her eyes.

He'd found a wall to lean his shoulders against, looking nonchalant and unbelievably sleek and exclusive. He didn't even have a single hair out of place.

'Leo?' A whisper was all she could manage as she stared in shaky disbelief at the tall figure, cataloguing every detail of his patrician features, every shift of expression on his face. It was still all angles and intriguing hollows, with strong classic features creating a miracle of symmetry. Looking at him acted like a trip switch that turned her brain off as she experienced a weird collision of past and present.

Seeing him that last time, the hurt and disillusion in his face before he'd walked away, had always stuck with her. There was no hurt now; his dark eyes were shuttered, stance relaxed, though there was a telltale tension in his flexing jawline that some might miss. But she knew that face so well, or at least a younger version of it, that she didn't miss anything. Not the tiny scar by the side of his mouth—she remembered tracing it with her finger—nor the waves of sinful male magnetism that poured off him.

A debilitating weakness slid through her and she wrapped her arms around herself as if that would keep the tight ball of her suppressed emotions in place. She was shivering despite the tendrils of heat that were breaking out across her skin, leaving a fiery trail.

Leo was there—impossible but a fact, the same but different. Nine years had built muscle, hardened the lines of his extraordinary, fascinating face, with its broad forehead, sharp commanding nose, a mouth that was all sin... and eyes that felt as though they were reaching into your soul.

She recognised, as her brain kicked into life, that it

was better to acknowledge this was nothing more than sexual attraction. Admittedly on an atomic scale, but it was all just hormones and chemical reactions.

Nothing more.

Of all the things she could have said—should have said—she heard herself gasp accusingly, 'You speak Italian!'

His lips quirked and her traitorous stomach flipped. 'It seemed only polite to learn my mother's tongue.'

'Of course—congratulations. It must be nice to have family.'

'That must have hurt.'

She shook her head, struggling to make sense of the tangle of emotions flooding her thoughts. Shaking her head, she said, 'I don't understand what you mean by that...'

'It could have been your family too—that must have hurt.'

An angry retort trembled on her tongue, but then she remembered her father's reaction to the news. 'I was happy for you, whether you believe it or not.'

'Most people would say you do sincerity very well.'

'Did you hurt them, those youths?' She needed a moment's reprieve from thinking about the past and Leo's clear scorn for her.

'We had a civilised conversation and they left. There's no need to thank me.'

His devil-may-care wide white grin did not extend to his eyes, framed by the dark, dense, curling lashes.

'I won't. I had it under control.' She saw something that could have been surprise flicker in the inky blackness of his eyes and lifted her chin a little higher.

'Yes, I saw that.'

She ignored the sarcastic jibe. 'Well, I don't know why you are here, but I don't believe in coincidences, so…?'

'Then you have changed, because you used to believe in the Easter bunny,' he ground out, his hard expression countering the pretend amazement in his voice.

'It's been nine years. Of course I've changed, Leo.' She had not let herself say or even think his name in that time. Excluding her dreams; she'd had to cut herself some slack where her subconscious was involved.

She would have known him, his voice, in pitch darkness, but he had changed too, she realised as she took in the minute details, looking up at him through her lashes and noting the power in his broader leather-covered shoulders.

The fact he looked slick, polished and expensive, attired head-to-toe in designer labels, did nothing to lessen the sheer force of him that had captivated her the first time she'd seen him all those years ago. Now there was an additional layer, an overall hardness to everything about him. Not just the planes of his superbly, *austerely* beautiful face, but in his stance. He carried himself with an arrogance that had not been there nine years ago. He exuded the absolute confidence of a male in the prime of his life who knew he was right at the top of the food chain.

The illicit shudders that shamefully ripped through her body as she stared up at him were no less primal than they had been that very first time she'd set eyes on Leo. She acknowledged the fact with a stab of self-disgust, but took comfort from the fact she was no longer running recklessly towards the excitement he represented. Despite the shameful heat between her legs, *she* had changed.

She knew about consequences.

Giving him up had been the hardest, most painful thing she'd ever had to do. Watching him walk away from her, thinking that she had betrayed him, had added an extra layer to that pain.

And now she had no idea what was in his head. His blank expression left her totally off-balance and in the dark. He had become an unknown entity.

He had always been, and still was, beautiful—the most beautiful thing she had ever seen—but the lanky, coltish quality he'd possessed at twenty had hardened.

Exciting.

The word popped into her head unbidden and she lowered her lashes in a silky screen while she fought for composure, or something that passed for it.

His presence was more disturbing than the young thugs he had seen off, but in a very different way.

Leo watched as she straightened her spine and lifted her head, cloaked in a coolness that didn't fool him. It amused him to think she imagined he couldn't see it for what it was—barely even skin-deep.

Amy was reacting to him the way she always had. Nine years was a long time, but it hadn't taught her how to conceal the fact that she was lusting after him.

'You should have given them your phone!'

For a split second his cloaked expression fell away and she could see his anger, hot enough to make her take an involuntary step backwards.

He clamped his lips tightly, as if to hold back further remonstrations, but his gaze continued to move over her face, studying each feature with disturbing intensity, travelling from her neck to her chin and lingering on her mouth before finally settling on her eyes.

She didn't react; indeed, she barely registered his words. The impact, the impossibility of him being there, the stream of questions tumbling through her head, made it a struggle to maintain a façade of anything even approaching calm.

Her tongue flickered across her dry lips, drawing his eyes and an inarticulate sound from his throat.

The noise jolted her free of her trance as her gaze shifted from his face to the phone he'd picked up, which he was now holding out to her.

'You were willing to fight for it, so take it.'

She ignored the sarcastic reminder and reached out, a deep shudder running though her body as their fingers grazed for a split second. Her eyes darted everywhere but at the face of the man she had once loved as she closed her fingers over the phone and brought it up tight against her chest.

Loved and left.

It had taken her months after that fateful night to stop reimagining the scene, replacing the facts with alternative outcomes, but none of the other scenarios had a particularly happy conclusion either.

Some people were just not meant to be together.

She tipped her head awkwardly in acknowledgement. Her eyes lifted as she shook her head and forced her lips into a smile. Not a great smile and it hurt, but she was definitely smiling, which was better than the alternative—which was gibbering incoherence.

'My whole life is on this phone...' Her attempt at a

laugh didn't work out brilliantly and his only response was a scowl.

'Your life!' He expelled the words through gritted teeth. 'Walking alone at this time of night in an area like this doesn't suggest too much concern for your life!'

'This area is perfectly—' She stopped and took a deep breath, recognising that arguing with him wasn't going to de-escalate a situation that needed some serious de-escalation. 'Look, I'm grateful, but I could have handled it. I was handling it.'

'Oh, is that a fact?'

This fresh display of blatant sarcasm brought a faint flush to her pale cheeks.

'Yes!' she retorted, pausing and trying to stick a hair-pin back into her once neat braid, which immediately tumbled back down. So much for dignity.

How dare he comment on where she ran her business, where she lived her life? Him, with his new family, his new life—he knew nothing of hers any more.

She flung the unravelling braid over her shoulder and cleared her throat. 'Sorry. Obviously, I am grateful, but I just…' She swallowed convulsively as emotion rose in her throat, thickening her words and, worse, bringing the sting of tears to her eyes. 'I just want to go home now.'

Aware that her voice had risen to a shrill plaintive wail, she took a deep breath, calming in theory but less so in reality. She cleared her throat again. 'This is just all a bit *weird*. You, here? Looking like this…' Her voice stalled. She fought the urge to say something daft like *Do you work out?* and said nothing at all.

'You have no security?'

The taut condemnation in his voice wrenched an

ironic laugh from her. His comment showed just how far removed this man was from the Leo she had known.

'Sure. It's their day off.' She studied his face; he *used* to have a sense of humour. 'Seriously, this is normally a quiet time of night, and I've taken self-defence classes.' She hadn't, but she didn't want him to know his criticism had got to her.

'You did?' He raised his eyebrows in challenge. She could tell he'd seen straight through her falsehood.

Sometimes it was irritating that she couldn't follow through with a perfectly good lie.

'No, but I intend to when I have the time, and I've read a lot of self-help books.'

'What, to whack little shits across the head with?'

She laughed and she didn't know why, because laughter in this situation was not a sane reaction, but for a second he had sounded so like the Leo she had once known that a wistful sigh left her lips. Before reality came flooding back in and she realised that he was no more like the old Leo than she was the old Amy. They never could be. It was time to say goodbye, once and for all.

CHAPTER THREE

'LOOK, THANKS FOR your help but—'

'Get in.'

'What?' Until the long, sleek designer car they were standing beside bleeped, she had no idea they had been walking while they talked. He had basically been herding her like a sheep as they spoke and she hadn't even noticed.

'I was always told not to get into cars with strangers,' she said, trying to inject some levity, admittedly strained, into the situation.

'I'm not a stranger, Amy.'

Her head tilted to look him full in the face.

Yes, he was.

It was as if he had been stripped back to a shell and rebuilt as a harder, scarier version of the Leo she had known and loved.

'The Tube—you can walk me to the Tube. That's it.' It was a meeting him midway offer that he appeared not to recognise.

'It's either home or the police station,' he said in a voice that left no room for negotiation. She was starting to suspect it was the norm for this Leo.

'Police?'

'To report the attack and theft.'

'I still have my phone and they won't class it as a mugging, so what would be the point?'

'You sound like an expert.'

She shook her head. 'I'm just stating the obvious.'

'In what world is that obvious?'

'My world, Leo.' But no longer his.

He said something in Italian and looked at her oddly.

'We can stand here arguing all day or you can get in.'

'Night,' she corrected, adding, 'not day.'

He looked bewildered and utterly vexed by her pedantic insertion. She took a deep breath and weighed her limited options.

'All right,' she said, sliding into the leather seat and sinking into the padded luxury that swallowed her up.

It probably made her shallow, but she missed that part of having money—the comfort, the space, the security and the *smell* of luxury. She inhaled, and Leo's scent hit her. Warm, clean, male. With an elusive hint of an undeniably expensive fragrance.

The engine was silent so when the car moved off she gave a little gasp of shock. 'Don't you want to know where I live?'

He flashed her a look before pulling out into the traffic. 'I know where you live, Amy.'

That could have sounded sinister… Actually, there was no *could* about it, it *was* sinister.

'Now,' he said, flashing her a smile that didn't reach his eyes, 'isn't this more comfortable than the Tube?'

She could lie and tell him that no, she would feel more comfortable packed in like a sardine with her face in someone's armpit. It wouldn't even be a total lie. Being in a confined space with this version of Leo was proving to be just as stressful. On a much deeper, chemical level.

Luckily, he didn't feel the need to make conversation because she was not capable of it. She sat there with a dazed look on her face as he drove, trying to build up some resistance to the aura of maleness he exuded. Trying not to tax her sex-whacked brain as she struggled to work out how he'd just happened to be passing by.

Obviously, he hadn't just happened to be passing by. This had all been planned. But what, exactly, was he planning now?

By the time he drew up outside her apartment block, she virtually threw herself out of the car.

He followed her. 'I'll see you in.'

If this had been an argument she could have won, she'd have fought it. But she knew resistance would be futile. She wouldn't win, not against *this* Leo.

To regain any amount of control she could, she avoided the lift in favour of the stairs. Being alone in a small space with him wasn't wise right now. She wasn't about to make that mistake twice.

He wasn't subtle when he strode straight past her into the living room of the flat before she'd barely opened the door. Her nostrils flared in annoyance. He was invading her space but she was in control, she reminded herself. She clung with bloodless fingers to the illusion.

'So, you live here alone?'

Her lips quirked into an ironic smile as she directed a look at her uninvited guest, who was taking in every detail of her home. Maybe he was thinking of when she had smuggled him into the Manor when her parents were absent, no doubt enjoying the fact that she was no longer living in the lap of luxury.

'I think maybe you know I don't, Leo.' He knew where she lived so it wasn't such a massive jump to assume he knew that her father lived here too.

He shrugged. 'Is your father around?'

'He's away for the weekend.' She caught her full lower lip between her teeth and tried to disguise her worry about the situation beneath a shrug and a smile.

Her dad had been cagey when she had challenged him about where he was going, and who with, adding another hurt, *'Don't you trust me?'* to end the discussion. Because actually, no, she didn't trust him, but there was no question of her voicing the fact. Her father was vulnerable; he had already tried to take his life once, and she hadn't been there for him.

He needed support, not a guilt trip, she reminded herself. He'd done his time.

'Why are you here, Leo? Nothing about this is accidental, is it?' she charged.

'You think I arranged for you to be attacked?'

'Of course not! But you weren't just passing either, were you?'

'True.' He performed a ninety-degree turn. 'This is a nice place.'

Her eyes narrowed and she couldn't bear it any longer. 'Stop it! Why not say what you mean? How the mighty have fallen! Enjoy the moment, that's fine! I guess I owe you that.' She extended her arms wide in invitation. 'If you must know, even this place is more than I can really afford, but Dad...' She bit her lip and shook her head, wondering why she had volunteered this much information.

'Wouldn't enjoy slumming it?'

Her eyes slid from his intuitive dark stare. Her father had made his opinion of the flat very clear, and it hadn't been positive!

'When will he be back?'

Amy continued to shrug off the inappropriately thick coat to reveal a pale blue denim shirt tied at the waist. Her jeans were a shade darker and clung to her thighs and when she bent down to unzip the ankle boots she was wearing the fabric pulled distractingly tight across her firm, rounded bottom. Her waist-length glossy hair, which was working its way loose of the braid, fell over one shoulder as she straightened up and kicked off the soft ankle boots she wore.

Leo was still struggling to take control of the testosterone-charged heat in his groin when she lifted her head.

'Monday,' she said, giving the knot at her waist an extra sharp tug. 'Like I already explained to you, he's away for the weekend, staying with friends.' Her hands landed on her hips as her chin lifted to a defensive angle, drawing his attention to the narrowness of her waist and the curve of her hips. Her supple, streamlined figure, the smooth curves of her body and her natural elegance had always made him think of a sleek cat. With claws, he added silently, thinking not just of the marks she had left on his shoulders on occasion, but the way she hadn't hesitated before cutting him out of her life. It was a good reminder of what he was here to do.

'Is this an interrogation?' she asked with a frown.

Leo looked at her and laughed again.

At eighteen, Amy hadn't had a clue about the sort of power her beauty gave her, let alone how use it to her own advantage. The fact that she still didn't amazed him.

'Have I said something funny?' she demanded, the hoarse note of belligerence in her voice shaking loose a memory—a memory of that throaty little whimper, low in her throat, she would let out when he kissed her, promptly negating any control he'd ever had around her.

'You're very touchy, *cara*.' He shifted his stance slightly to ease the ache in his groin.

A man might ask himself at this point just who was being punished here, he thought, permitting himself a flicker of an ironic self-mocking smile.

'I'm not.'

It might be a piece of poetic justice, his plan to rub her little nose in their flipped fortunes by bringing her into his world, allowing her to see what she had missed out on, but he hadn't factored in the fact that she wouldn't be the only one made to feel uncomfortable with the arrangement. She was still the most incredibly sensual woman he had ever met.

Amy, reacting to the tension buzzing in the air like static, closed her eyes, bringing her lashes down to act like a glossy but inadequate protective shield, casting a shadow across her high smooth cheeks. It was then that he noted the purple smudges under her soft brown eyes.

'Do you ever sleep?'

She shrank under his critical stare, clearly suddenly aware of what a wreck she looked. So different from the flawlessly glossy women he was used to escorting.

'Thank you for your concern, but being self-employed means I need to put in the hours, and I like being my own boss.'

The look she gave him suggested that wasn't entirely true. But he didn't care to explore it further. He was more interested in furthering his cause.

'Do you like your father's new friends?'

It took Amy a moment to retrieve the thread he had picked back up. Where was he going with this? Why did he want to know?

'*New* friends—?'

'Well, I doubt if many of his old golf club buddies hung around, and you said he was away with friends.'

'After he was…arrested…' she silently mocked herself for the small tell-tale hesitation '…we were toxic, but who needs friends like that, anyway?' she countered with a shrug, thinking miserably that her father needed them, he desperately needed them, his old life, the club memberships and committees.

Leo just shrugged and, not for the first time, Amy wondered how he had become so invulnerable. Hard as steel.

'But not you—you stood by him,' he stated.

Amy's glance slid from his. She remembered, all too well, wishing that she could walk away. 'He's my father. I know he's not perfect.' And she also knew how vulnerable he was.

Leo's harsh, mocking laugh brought an angry flush to her cheeks. Partly because of the guilt she felt at not having been there, not in a way that counted, when her father *had* needed her. She'd been too angry with him to guess the level of his desperation.

Leo responded with an infuriating languid half smile as he walked over to the mantelpiece above the electric fire and peered at the photos that lined it.

'So you haven't always been afraid of horses,' he said, picking up one of a curly-haired child sitting on top of a chunky pony, holding a rosette. 'You used to be a lot fairer.'

Her hand went automatically to her hair, despising that she cared what she looked like in this moment.

'No, that's not me, and I'm not afraid of horses.' She loved horses but the bargain had been that she was allowed to help out at the stables, but she must never get on a horse.

Having lost one daughter in a riding accident, the ban had not been that surprising. Amy had understood why her parents were overprotective, but that didn't make it any easier to accept the restrictions. Restrictions that had made her the odd one out growing up, because it hadn't just been the horse-riding her parents had deemed dangerous; there were so many other things she'd never got to do either, no sleepovers, no camping trips. The list of things she had not been allowed to do had seemed endless.

She hadn't told Leo about Alice back then, about why she'd felt she had to be the perfect daughter. Good enough for both herself and the child they'd lost.

But, of course, she never had been. Had Alice been perfect? Would it have been different if her sister had grown up, become a rebellious teen first? But Alice hadn't. She'd never flunked a maths test, never had a teenage strop or an unsuitable boyfriend.

Long before she'd met Leo, Amy had stopped competing with the perfect ghost of her sibling, and stopped trying to make her parents proud, recognising it wasn't possible.

Leo, of course, was an excellent horseman. One of the first times she'd seen him he'd been on horseback, and she'd been riveted. Watching the tall stranger, as he'd been then, on the frisky half-schooled mare.

Her stomach flipped and quivered as she recalled the shocking impact, the visceral reaction she had experienced. Sexual attraction that she had been too inexperienced to hide.

She snatched the picture from his hand and replaced it on the mantelpiece. 'It's not me—it's my sister, Alice,' she said, straightening the photo frame.

'You have a sister?' The furrow between his brows deepened. 'Older, I'm assuming?'

'She would have been.'

An alert expression slid into his eyes. 'She died.'

It was a statement, and one she didn't respond to.

'You miss her?'

'I never knew her.' Reacting to what might have been pity in his voice—pity she didn't want or need—she responded more sharply than she'd intended. Softening it, she added, 'It happened ten years before I was born. My parents were no longer young when I was born; for the first six months she was pregnant with me, Mum thought she was experiencing the menopause.'

'You never mentioned you had a sister.'

Amy felt a wave a guilt, remembering how good it had felt to be with someone who didn't bring her dead sister into the conversation at every opportunity, who didn't compare her with the ghost.

'I'm sure there were things you didn't tell me.' There were a lot of things she hadn't told him, and then suddenly there had been nothing to tell him.

No baby.

Nine years later and the thought of her miscarriage still came with the same pain. She ignored the tight feeling in her chest and the dull ache.

Revisiting the past wouldn't help anyone. Least of all her.

'You weren't just passing, Leo, so what's this all about?'

'So how old was your sister when she died?'

She sighed out her frustration when he ignored her question.

'She was ten.'

She glanced at another photo of a curly blonde cherubic smiling baby. 'They thought I might get fairer as I got older, but I never did. I got darker, except for—' She touched the blonde streak that sprang from her forehead that no one ever believed was natural.

'So where are you?' he asked, scanning the gallery line-up of photos, seeing the same child at various ages, but none of a dark-haired child.

'Oh, no one prints out their online photos these days.' Especially if you never quite lived up to expectation, she thought, dodging his eyes, determined not to allow him to spotlight her insecurities. He was no longer twenty, no longer in love with her. He didn't get to know about her insecurities.

Suddenly, she felt every month of her twenty-eight years, and it was hard to think that she'd ever been so happy, living in the moment and never thinking ahead.

It wouldn't have worked.

It *couldn't* have worked.

Unbidden, the memory of Leo standing outside her family home, his hand reaching out to her, drifted into her head. For a split second she was back on that emotional ledge, wanting to take his hand and knowing it was impossible.

The look on Leo's lean face…the expression in his dark eyes under his long messy fringe had been so intense and real as he'd willed her to take the hand he held outstretched to her…was spotlit in her memory, every detail frozen in time.

She shook her head and she saw the realisation of what she'd been seeing in her mind's eye slide into his gaze in the shift of muscle as his jaw clenched.

She took a deep breath and dragged herself back to the present. 'Look, we have established you were not just passing. That's not to say I'm not grateful you got me out of that situation, but really…'

'You realise the more you tell me how grateful you are, the less grateful you sound?' he observed, sounding amused.

'Why, Leo? If you are here to see how the mighty have fallen, well, that's fair enough. I suppose I deserve that, but not Dad. He's an old man trying hard to rebuild his life. So if you're just here to tell me how great your life is going, that's fine. You're about to be married…

You've won the lottery… Whatever it is, good luck for the future, and goodbye.'

Not that he needed luck, from what she had read.

She held open the door, anxious for this farce to be over.

'Actually, I'm here to offer you a job.'

CHAPTER FOUR

THE SILENCE STRETCHED.

'Me, work for you?' She stared at him, her eyebrows hitting her hairline. 'Have you been drinking?'

'No, but if you're offering…?'

Her lips tightened. 'I'm not,' she retorted unsmilingly. 'Unless it's escaped your notice, I already have a job.'

'I imagine it must be tough coming down in the world—a hard landing.'

She lifted her chin. 'I'm not complaining.'

'Your margins must be very tight.'

She stayed silent, likely sensing something was coming. The *something* made her visibly tense in anticipation.

'What I'm suggesting is temporary.' Long enough to enjoy the satisfaction of seeing her in *his* world, out of her depth. Because, despite the fact that she had lost everything, she had retained the innate attitude of a winner. Where the hell did her strength come from?

He pushed away the stab of admiration that came with the thought, focusing instead on the inexplicable way she had defended her father. When she wanted to fight for something, she did so like a tigress.

Yet she hadn't fought for him.

Amy shook her head and gave him a stubborn blank look.

'I need a chef for an upcoming event.'

'Is that meant to be a joke?' She pointed to her face. 'I am not laughing. There are a lot of chefs out there, Leo.'

'It's a tough gig and I understand if you don't feel up to the challenge.'

'It isn't a matter of feeling up to anything. Nothing in the world would make me work for a man who...'

'Was your social inferior?'

The colour flew to her cheeks. 'I wasn't going to say that.'

'It's true, though.'

'You never forgave me, did you?'

'I almost forgot you existed,' he lied without hesitation.

She flinched, but after a split second and a convulsive swallow she lifted her chin.

There was a reason why Leo had risen to the heights he had, a reason why the business world revered him. His ruthlessness was unrivalled, so it was infuriating that he felt the need to remind himself that *nothing* about Amy was authentic, not the bitten lip or the unshed tears.

'And then your father's case hit the headlines, and you stayed a daddy's girl to the end. It reminded me that we have unfinished business, Amy.' He paused, his contemptuous dark eyes narrowed, trained on her face for a long moment before he asked, 'Are you, Amy?'

The lethally soft question made her shiver. 'Am I what?'

'A daddy's girl. What would you do for your father? How far does your devotion and blind loyalty go?'

'What do you mean?' she asked, even though she was pretty sure she didn't want to know.

'We have established that working for me is not something that sets your soul alight with joy. The question is, would you work for me in order to save your father from another stint in jail? For a second offence, he might not have the option of an open prison.'

The possibility that he wasn't bluffing sent an icy chill through Amy. In her mind, she could see the scattered pills on the floor amidst empty bottles and her father's body on the floor, unmoving. She knew with total certainty that if faced with that shame again, he wouldn't get as far as prison.

'He's not going back to prison.' Amy could hear the note of panic in her voice. 'He's turning his life around.'

Leo refused to recognise the stab of guilt that speared him when he saw the fear in her eyes—that, at least, was authentic. 'Those new friends your father made behind bars, they have friends on the outside who have large quantities of cash made illegally, which they need to launder through a legitimate business.' He arched a speculative ebony brow. 'Have your accounts been looking more healthy of late?'

She looked at him, loathing shining in her eyes, hating how what he was saying made sense. 'How do you know any of this?'

'It's easy to *know* things when you know where to look. Your father is not a master criminal, although in his arrogance and greed I'm quite sure he thinks he is.' His voice dropped to a foreboding purr as he tilted his head and scanned her face with a clinical detachment that made her feel like a bug under a microscope. 'Are you in on the scam, Amy?'

She stepped forward and lifted her arm in the same moment. The action was pure reflex and she barely registered what she was about to do until fingers like steel wrapped around her wrist.

Her eyes widened in shocked horror, which was supplanted when instead of releasing her hand he dragged her towards him. He bent his head and she literally stopped breathing, her eyes drifting closed as his head lowered.

The warmth of his breath on her palm sent a shiver through her body and then she was free. Apart from the tangled emotions churning inside her as she rubbed her palm hard against her thigh.

She made herself meet his gaze. His taunting smile made it obvious he knew she had thought he was going to kiss her.

The only question was, did he also know she had wanted him to?

'What do you want, Leo?' she asked, making her voice cold, even though it did nothing to lower her internal temperature.

'I've already told you I need a chef… I think a six-week contract will suffice.'

Six weeks of working for him and he would have the satisfaction of seeing her fail. Amy would be begging to leave; she had developed unexpected steel, but in a war of attrition there was only one winner.

'My business…?'

'I will pay for a temp to fill in for you. I am assuming that your alcoholic helper will be able to cope without you.'

Anger blazed in her soft eyes as she drew herself up to her full height. 'How do you—' she began and stopped. It was pointless to ask why Leo's position gave him a reach that she couldn't even begin to imagine. 'Ben hasn't had a drink in ten years and he is my business partner, equal partners. He put money in, and his knowledge has made all the difference.'

'An older man to lean on,' he mused, pressing a finger to his chin. 'Am I seeing a pattern here…?'

'My father is trying hard—'

'To do what, exactly? Set himself up as the go-to man for drug dealers with some cash to launder?'

The blood drained from her face, the colour change so dramatic that any doubts that she had any involvement in George's extracurricular activities vanished.

'Drugs?' she stuttered out. 'He wouldn't!' Hearing the question in her own voice, she rounded on him furiously. 'I suppose you don't believe in second chances.'

'I believe they're wasted on most people.'

'God, when did you get so cynical?' she flared.

'I think you can take some credit for that, *cara*.'

He managed to make the endearment sound like a mocking insult. 'Stop calling me that!' she hissed in frustration.

'I'll take that as a yes, shall I?' He smiled and turned towards the door, pausing as he swung back. 'Oh, and as my employee I think a bit of courtesy might be in order for our working relationship.'

She lowered herself into a mocking curtsey.

'I'll have the contract sent over for you to sign.'

'What, in blood?' she snarled.

He laughed and she remembered a time when his smile had not been an exercise in cynicism. Remembering all the times he had teased her and made her laugh, she was seized by a quite crazy sense of loss.

She had lost Leo years ago.

'We leave on Friday.'

She shook her head, her brow pleated in a perplexed frown. 'Friday? Where to?'

'For Tuscany.'

'Tuscany in Italy?'

He arched a brow and regarded her as if she'd just made a totally facile comment.

'That's too soon. I will have things to—'

He brushed aside her objections. 'You don't have to do anything except just be ready. You do have an up-to-date passport?' he asked, already moving through the door.

She nodded and he was gone.

CHAPTER FIVE

FRIDAY CAME AND as Amy sat waiting with her bag packed she began to wonder again if this had all been an elaborate hoax. It had the hallmarks of an elaborate 'gotcha' for someone who had too much time on his hands. He wasn't going to show; she was just going to sit here all day.

She had signed the contract, not in blood but in black ink. Not that it had made the act any easier. Before she had signed the next six weeks of her life away, she had confronted her father, hoping, *willing* him to deny everything, tell her this was some terrible mistake.

It wasn't a mistake, it was the truth, and almost as shocking as his eventual admission after a lot of waffle was his utter lack of remorse, the way he had taken no responsibility at all for his actions.

Reminding herself that he was vulnerable, she had held tight to her anger and the seething sense of betrayal while taking in his reaction to being challenged. His mood shifting from initial shock and denial to indignation, to the inevitable tearful hurt.

She had stood by him throughout his trial and sentence, she'd been there when he got out, and he'd not only lied to her, he'd used her. Things were at the point where the only option was to call him out on his manipulative behaviour or physically remove herself from the scene before she said something that she would regret.

She had walked away knowing that a lot of what her father did was an act, but the fragility was real. If something she said, even a true something, pushed her father to another suicide attempt she would never be able to live with the guilt.

Was the promise she had extracted from her father worth anything? She wanted to believe that he would end his association with his shady friends. *She could only hope.*

Every night since she had signed away her immediate future she had barely slept and, when she did, she woke up in a cold sweat. That was bad enough, but the hot sweats when she woke aching, yelling Leo's name, were infinitely worse. When even her father, not the most observant of men, asked her if she was ill, she knew that the sleepless nights were showing.

Or maybe it was living with the knowledge that she was still attracted to Leo, a man who now hated her enough to blackmail her. It was a terrible, wicked thing to do, and she wanted to hate him for it. And she did, but at the same time she kind of thought she deserved it; she had not set out to make him hate her, but she could see why he did. She had broken his heart.

Small wonder that she tried to focus on the basics and let the deeper meaning sort itself out. Basics being thinking about Tuscany, an exciting test of her skills, and she did love a challenge.

The challenge, she suspected, was not going to be culinary but emotional. It was one thing to empathise with Leo's take on the situation; it was quite another to allow him to grind her down and make her doubt her own ability, which she suspected was his game plan.

Amy was sure that the next weeks would be much simpler to navigate if she could return that hate, but instead she was fatally attracted to him.

It was eleven-thirty when her doorbell finally rang. Her father had gone for coffee with an old friend who he had reconnected with, and his mood had been ebullient when they had parted. So she hadn't needed to invent a reason for him not to be there.

Luckily, he had accepted the basic facts she had supplied—she'd accepted a short and well-paid contract, having been recommended by a former colleague. He hadn't pressed for the details, and Amy had not filled him in.

She had wondered what his reaction would be if he knew that Leo would be her boss. Would he be furious and go into meltdown at the suggestion? Or—and actually this was the worse option—would he see an opportunity for her to pick up where they'd left off? The fact that Leo Romano was now mega-rich no doubt made him a lot more acceptable to George Sinclair.

Either way, she didn't want to know.

A middle-aged man, suited and booted, stood there.

'Miss Sinclair.' His smile was polite and friendly. 'I'm here to take you to the airport.' He saw her looking past him. 'Mr. Romano is already in Italy and he will meet us at the airport. These your bags?'

'Yes—oh, no, I can manage.'

He ignored her and picked them up. 'You travel light.'

The man carrying her bags walked ahead to a gleaming limo taking up several parking spaces.

Amy paused at the door being held open, butterflies rioting in her stomach.

What are you doing, Amy?

The driver spoke, and the sound jolted her, cutting through her paralysing apprehension.

She blinked, having no idea what he'd said, but she managed a half smile and nodded, taking a steadying breath before she slid inside the luxurious interior. The door was closed silently behind her, but to Amy it sounded like the clanging of a metal prison door.

She reminded herself that she wasn't a prisoner, she was here of her own volition. She didn't need an escape plan—six weeks, that was all. Six weeks was nothing.

To distract herself she began silent calculations of how many days, hours, minutes were involved in six weeks and barely noticed the route they took through London.

'We are here.'

The information relayed through the intercom made her start. She focused on slowing her galloping heart rate while the driver parked up, and waited while he went around to open the passenger door.

'When is the flight?' she asked, pleased that she sounded calm and in control.

The driver looked at her oddly. 'Take-off is in about ten minutes.'

Amy couldn't understand how he appeared so calm. The last time she had flown, she had arrived three hours ahead of time and still nearly missed her flight. Then the penny dropped.

'This is a private airport,' she realised, taking in her surroundings.

'That's right.'

'And that's a private plane?' The question was redundant as the jet on the runway had *Romano* in gold written along its wings.

If she'd been less nervous and apprehensive about what awaited her, she would have enjoyed the flight with her every whim being catered for. Not that she had many whims, other than a deep desire for no turbulence.

That wish was granted.

Amy, still on the receiving end of VIP treatment when they landed, wondered if the smiles would stop if they knew she was just the cook. She didn't test the theory but her entourage deserted her completely anyhow when a tall dynamic figure appeared.

Leo did not appear inclined to encourage the official groupies and after a brief exchange he made his way to her side.

'Good flight?'

It was such a normal thing to say in an abnormal situation that she almost laughed, though it seemed doubtful if she could have forced anything past the emotional occlusion in her throat.

She gave a tiny tip of her head, which seemed adequate.

'Do you want a transfer or will you walk?'

'You live close by?'

'To the helipad.' He looked at her sharply as she blanched. 'Is that an issue?'

'No, not at all,' she lied stoically. If he wanted to see

her fall apart he would have to do better than a chopper ride.

They had been airborne for ten minutes before he spoke. 'You do know your eyes are closed?'

'Well, it didn't happen accidentally.'

'You don't like helicopters?'

'They are delightful on the ground.'

She opened one eye and saw that he was laughing and looking far too human and ridiculously attractive.

'Sadistic bastard,' she muttered, perhaps a little louder than she had intended.

She kept her eyes closed until she sensed the sharp descent. Her curiosity finally overcoming her fear, her eyes blinked open. Her stomach flip was nothing to do with the distance from the ground but the dark eyes that were watching her. How long their gaze stayed connected she had no idea, but she blinked first, just before her internal temperature had reached a critical point.

'Oh, my God!' She blinked at the sheer scale of the building that dominated the landscape. The view from the air was even more impressive than the one she had seen online. 'It's a real castle.'

'What did you expect, a flatpack? Actually, it's more of a fortified manor, but the ramparts are still intact and the towers.'

'So beautiful it makes me wish I could paint.'

'It has been painted by many artists.'

She expected him to mock her for her sharp cry and her white knuckles on landing, but he displayed unexpected tact and pretended not to notice. Or then again, she mocked herself, maybe he wasn't as obsessed with her body language as she was with his.

'Our carriage awaits.'

The carriage turned out to be a Jeep, and her bags had already been thrown into the back when she climbed in beside them. Leo got in the front with the driver. The two men kept up a conversation in Italian as they drove into a courtyard.

She climbed out dragging a bag with her.

'Leave it; someone will bring them.'

He opened a door and Amy preceded him into the short corridor, lined with various stores and a cool room.

'Kitchen,' he said, pointing to the door ahead. Despite the closed door, the sounds of a noisy argument in full swing reached them.

Leo felt a stab of annoyance at the tickle of guilt he felt. He could have allowed her to settle in first after the flight, but the fact was he didn't *want* her to settle in.

It was irrational to feel guilt. This was the perfect situation to reveal the real Amy who hid under this new persona, the one that would run away when the going got tough. He just hadn't expected it to be *this* tough so soon.

Knuckles resting on the door, he pushed it in a couple of inches and was greeted by a particularly crude epithet and winced. Pained frown still in place, he glanced down, only to discover Amy was not looking shocked, more amused by his reaction if the twitching lips were any indication.

'Relax, Leo, I've heard worse. This is a kitchen, after all, although I must admit that is a new one on me. So inventive! I should have asked—who do I report to?'

'Me.'

She slung him a look. 'I mean, who is the head chef?'

'You are. I thought that was understood.'

The way he was watching her reminded her of a cat playing with its prey. Refusing to give him the satisfaction of seeing her fall apart, which was presumably the plan, she lifted her chin.

'Oh, I understand totally.'

Displaying a combination of self-possession and determination, she gave the high ponytail she wore in bouncy defiance a determined swish and lifted her chin before stepping into the room. Leo followed her. He had sat through many boardroom battles, but this was different, much more earthy. The blood on the walls in this argument might be tomato-based but it was all a lot more *real*.

Despite the fact that a full-scale war appeared to have broken out in the kitchen, Amy immediately felt some of the tension leave her shoulders. This was her world, and she took in at a glance a very well-equipped kitchen that any restaurant would have been proud of, though no kitchen she had ever worked in had ancient beams sitting cheek by jowl with the latest in culinary high-tech.

It was actually a relief to have something to distract her from the things that Leo's presence did to her. The prickle caused by the man who had guided her was still there, just under her skin, but her stomach had stopped its athletic flips and it was a relief to be able to split her focus and concentrate on something other than his dominating presence and, of course, her reaction to it.

Taking advantage of the fact that no one seemed to have noticed she was there, she allowed herself a few moments of invisibility to absorb the scene of general noisy chaos and diagnosed too many bosses, too many egos and an excess of testosterone. The ratio of male to female accounted for that, though she knew from personal experience that any woman here could give as good as they got.

First one person and then another noticed their visitors, until only the two main swaggering protagonists continued to eyeball each other, the noise now just the insults they were still hurling.

Amy put some extra distance between her and Leo, the action both professional and personal. She didn't want to be seen as part of the management, acknowledging that while not out of sight or out of mind, it helped her brain function to distance herself from all that undiluted masculinity.

'Don't look at him,' she said, thinking, *Excellent advice, Amy, take it yourself,* before inserting herself into the centre of the drama and adding in a soft, cool voice that nevertheless carried, 'I'm in charge.'

A ripple of shock moved through the room like a wave, leaving shocked silence in its wake. A silence broken by the sound of liquid boiling over from a pan, sending plumes of steamy acrid smoke into the air.

Amy strode over to the stove and switched off the gas, directing a frowning stare into the contents of the pan while muttering. She slid a sly sideways glance in Leo's direction. *'He* wouldn't know a remoulade from a roulade.'

Someone laughed, which Amy, ever the optimist, took as a good sign.

'Right.' She swung back with a smile that gave no hint of the fact that her heart was hammering against her ribs, or the fact that the tall figure she had just mocked had his obsidian stare fixed like a laser on her.

She didn't wilt. Instead, she channelled the adrenaline.

'I'm Amy and…well, we can do the introductions later,' she continued briskly, waving a hand around the room before walking across to a board where a menu was pinned and took it down. 'So—' her eyes flashed from the paper to the tall lanky man who had been at the centre of the disagreement '—dinner, for how many?'

'Thirty,' a voice supplied.

'And the issue you were arguing over is…?'

'I ordered lobster and this…'

'I ordered what you said, and you said crab—'

Because the two men looked ready to face off again, Amy spoke over them.

'Always annoying when there's an order mix-up,' she agreed with a *been there, done that* sigh. 'I worked with an Italian guy who used to say *granchio* when he made a mistake—it means crab, doesn't it?'

There were several nods of agreement and several grins in recognition of the irony.

Someone threw out a remark in Italian.

'Sorry, guys, my Italian is purely culinary based. English and French are my limit. I love that challenge, don't you, to use the ingredients at hand? I remember when I couldn't make the chilli crab salsa to top a pea risotto that I had planned. Of course, the crabs arrived too late, which is typical.' She paused to allow the mutter of rueful agreement. 'But the coconut crab rice the next day proved a massive hit, and it actually became our signature dish.

'As the newbie and as we're on the clock, how about I'm the runner tonight? Any spare whites?' Amy asked, teasing her ponytail into a knot and producing extra pins to secure it there.

'Not that would fit you, Chef.'

Someone shook out a black apron. 'Will this do for tonight?'

'Perfect!'

Leo watched as the diminutive figure wrapped the apron strings three times around her narrow waist and smiled sunnily at her audience before she picked up the hot handle of the burnt copper saucepan using a cloth.

'How about I put this pan in to soak and make another batch of...' she arched a brow and picked up a bottle off the counter '...Marsala sauce?' Amy said, picking up another bottle that lay beside a work station, glancing at the label with an approving nod before applying herself to a pile of shallots.

She was well aware that her knife skills were being marked out of ten by her audience. But as she was quietly confident that she was a twelve and a half out of ten, she was not bothered by the scrutiny.

After everyone had begun to drift away to quietly take up their own tasks, Leo watched her for a few more moments in silence. The other staff gave him some wary glances that managed to convey he was in the way. Amy, completely immersed in her task, appeared to have tuned him out completely.

His chagrin at the situation held a thread of self-mockery. He had orchestrated this and it had not produced the result he had anticipated. Far from finding herself thrown into a situation she couldn't cope with, Amy hadn't seemed even slightly stressed.

Cope? The woman had *conquered* without even raising her voice. She had turned his imagined scenario on its head. Instead of falling apart, she had calmly taken charge and seemed on the brink of winning over her very critical audience. An audience that had already managed to make three, that he knew of, very experienced chefs hang up their chef's hats and walk.

Avoiding someone who was wildly whipping something in a massive metal bowl, he moved to where Amy stood, receiving several slightly nervous but distracted head nods on the way.

'Don't you want to see your room, unpack?'

Amy threw him a quick, incredulous glance over her shoulder. 'Now?' Her astonishment at the suggestion shone in her soft brown eyes. 'I'm working, but fine, later…someone here can show me the way, I'm sure.'

Leo's jaw clenched, shock and outrage flashing cold in his eyes, then his sense of the ridiculous reasserted itself as he tried to remember the last time he had been dismissed.

When was the last time he had laughed at himself?

'Fine.'

Without looking at him, she waved a fluttering hand of dismissal.

His exercise in humiliation was not going to plan, but Leo was a long way from admitting defeat. Amy was in her element now, but there was a big difference between a dinner and the upcoming gala event.

His phone vibrated and he glanced at the caller identity, his mouth twitching into a smile as the image of a svelte six-foot blonde with a penchant for six-inch heels formed in his head. She was ambitious, voracious and enjoyed sex without emotional *mess,* as she called it.

He continued to walk, ignoring the call and shoving the phone back into his pocket, the image swiftly fading from his mind and replaced by the small dynamic figure he had just left in the kitchen.

The kitchen was the one room in this building where people didn't bow and scrape when he appeared, but today he had been totally invisible; there was another star shining too brightly. He had to admit to being surprised and, also albeit reluctantly, impressed.

Pretty hard not to admit that Amy had handled a room full of massive egos like a pro, which, of course, she was—a fact that was only just bedding in.

It might, he conceded, not be as easy as he had anticipated to make her want to run for cover. This Amy was not averse to a bit of manipulation herself... The acknowledgment made him smile. Though the smile faded as his thoughts made the leap to the other ways she might have changed and grown...and the people—the men in particular—who might have joined her on that journey.

Amy knew there could have been improvements—the chef basting the sirloin had been a bit stingy with the butter in her opinion—but the meal was apparently a success which, in this environment, seemed to amount to a win. Especially as Leo's grandfather was visiting, a figure who, reading between the lines, seemed to inspire awe rather than affection.

Amy was not someone who thought a kitchen worked better on fear, insults and a lot of curses thrown into the mix. As with any organisation, the message at the top filtered down. It did not make her feelings warm towards Leo, who was boss here.

A boss, she had been mournfully told, who didn't much care what he ate. He even came into the kitchen and made himself toast and things that he called sandwiches. She was amused by the complaints but hid it. It was always frustrating to cook for someone who thought of food as fuel and not a sensory experience.

Luckily, it seemed that he did entertain quite a lot when he was in residence. Amy wondered what this army of artists did when he wasn't, but she didn't want to stir up trouble so she kept her thoughts to herself.

It was fifteen minutes since the last of the staff had left at her suggestion. Her initial assessment was that they were a good bunch with a couple of personality clashes but nothing major.

Amy didn't mind the clean-up post service; she found it kind of relaxing. Sleeping straight after a tough service when her adrenaline was still high was hard, though a dinner party of thirty, no matter how indifferent to food artistry the host was, was not what she would class as tough.

She was cleaning the seals on the last fridge, an area too often missed, when she heard the door swing open.

'I'll be with you now,' she tossed out, assuming it was someone assigned to showing her to her room.

'Why are you cleaning? There are staff—'

Her stomach fluttering, she spun around so fast she almost lost her balance. She did lose a couple of hairgrips that fell with a gentle clatter onto the floor, and she immediately dropped to her knees and chased them, sticking them haphazardly back into her hair as she straightened up.

'What are you doing here?' She addressed the accusing question to the sinfully beautiful man dressed in a dinner jacket, his tie hanging loose, his broad shoulders propped against the wall as he stood there watching her.

His entire attitude seemed languid but his eyes were very alert and, now that she looked into them, she read annoyance and something else that she hastily skipped over in the ink-dark depths.

'More like, what are you doing here?' He noted the faint purple smudges beneath her eyes again and felt his aggravation rise. It was as if she was trying to make him feel guilty, but she wouldn't succeed, he decided, nursing his resentment. 'I brought you here for a tour of the kitchens, not to—'

Nostrils flared, she sucked in a deep breath. 'You brought me here to watch me become overwhelmed, maybe cry a few tears. Or were you expecting me to seek a strong masculine shoulder to weep on?'

Her eyes went of their own volition to the area under discussion just as his broad, muscle-packed shoulders left the wall and his physical presence became even more dominating.

'Sorry to disappoint,' she sneered. 'But you'll have to do better than that. I have worked in kitchens a hell of a lot tougher than this one.'

'I thought you were self-taught?'

The mockery in his voice was something she had heard before. 'I had no formal training, yes. My training was all hands-on. I learnt on the job and worked my way up.'

'I'm surprised Daddy allowed you to get your hands dirty.'

She laughed. 'Oh, he was about as contemptuous about me doing *menial* work as you.'

Outrage at being compared with George Sinclair flashed in his dark eyes. 'I have never termed any job as menial.'

His outraged stance was not exactly screaming equality and another time she might have laughed in his face, but she settled for saying, 'You don't need to, Leo, you have perfected the sneer.'

She might have been imagining it, but she thought her mocking admiration drew a low growl from him.

'*Dio!*' he cursed, seething through gritted teeth. As much as he would have liked to react to the provocative glitter in her golden-brown eyes, he refused. 'So there is something you care enough about to disobey your father.' Annoyed that she had pushed him into a retort that had revealed an open wound he would not own even to himself, he closed his eyes.

They stayed closed long enough to miss her flinch and the blood draining from her face.

'I was only nineteen, Leo.' *But I'm not now.* This was what he wanted—to get under her skin. Why let him see that he had succeeded?

'I am sorry if I hurt you back then.'

The sincerity shining in her face only fed his anger. Did she really think saying sorry made a difference now? Her attitude only hardened his resolve to see this thing through.

'It's ancient history.' He produced a dismissive shrug, comfortable with the lie that came easily. 'But I don't want to see you weep.' In his head, there was a line between retribution and bullying, and making a woman cry crossed that line—*any* woman, he emphasised for his own benefit.

Amy's response to the admission which seemed dragged out of him was a cynical little smile. 'But it would be a bonus?'

His tense jaw tightened another painful notch, her reaction making the guilt he had been fighting off throughout the evening with each successive course delivered to the appreciative diners even more irrational.

Her ability to play on his emotions was a weakness he had to acknowledge in order to guard against it.

'I'm sure you've found enough sympathy and a few protective shoulders to cry on over the years.'

She arched a brow. 'For the record, I do not gently crumble and cry out for strong masculine shoulders or even weak ones.' She narrowed her eyes to show her self-reliance, which was real.

If it hadn't been, she wouldn't be here today, it was that simple. She pushed away all the painful memories she had built a protective mental wall around—watching her mother fighting for her life, losing first Leo and then the baby Amy hadn't even known she'd conceived, her mother's death and then shortly afterwards her father's shameful conviction.

She lifted her chin and thought, *You're tough, Amy, so act like it.* 'If I did need a shoulder, it wouldn't be yours,' she declared and immediately wished the rather childish addition unsaid. It did rather shake her off her firm footing on the high ground.

She took a deep breath and, channeling a calm she was a million miles from feeling, continued. 'I am fulfilling my part of this deal and if it isn't as painful for me as you obviously hoped, that's tough! I am good at what I do.' She planted the spray she was still holding on the work surface and suddenly sagged, gripping the copper surface for support, her voice losing a little of the angry venom as she finished with a waspish, 'Sorry if that makes you unhappy, but it's a fact.' She swallowed. 'It's been a long day.' Then wished she hadn't added that because it sounded as if she was fishing for the sympathy vote.

'Have you actually eaten anything while you've been producing miraculous food?' he demanded, sounding less sympathetic and more annoyed.

Amy had decided the best way to deal with him was to maintain a snooty silence but her professional pride kicked in. '*Miraculous?*'

'Well, even my grandfather didn't complain. I think he actually said it was *quite nice,* and that in itself translates as miraculous.'

'Did you like it?' *Oh, God, I sound so needy.*

'Yes, I did. Sit down before you fall down, Amy.'

'I…'

A sound of hissing exasperation left his lips. Before she had any idea of his intention, he spanned her waist with his big hands and with a casual display of strength lifted her up onto the counter surface of the kitchen island, which should not have impressed her or made the heat unfurl in her belly.

It did both and she despised her weakness.

He was rifling through the contents of one of the fridges. 'There's nothing to eat,' he complained.

Despite herself, Amy laughed. 'I thought you liked the food.'

'It's not for me, it's for you—but I'm a big guy; I need quantity, not pretty.' She might be the exception, he admitted as his eyes travelled over her delicate features. She was a classic example of small but perfectly formed and just looking at her made him hungry. 'What's this?' he asked, turning his attention back to the fridge as he pulled off a cover and sniffed the contents of a large bowl.

'Oh, there were some chicken livers left over and I couldn't waste them, so I made a bit of paté.'

'A bit?' He eyed the massive bowl as he planted it on the work surface. 'Bread?' He walked to the huge terracotta crock and lifted the lid, pulling out a loaf.

'Yum, that treacle bread is just divine. Jamie has a gift, seriously, she does.'

'Who is Jamie?'

'The only female in the kitchen?' she said, her sarcasm losing its force as the level of surreal in this scenario finally hit her.

'Other than you.'

'Yes, I suppose so, but I don't count. I'm just your token blackmail victim.'

He turned his head as she swung her legs and yawned. He turned away quickly, but not before the image had set free a protective surge of emotion that he told himself was nine years out of date. He had wanted to protect her back then and she had thrown it back in his face.

Now, the person she needed protecting from was him.

'Who told you that you don't count?'

Amy couldn't have put a time stamp on the moment she'd realised that she would never really count. Nobody had said it outright, but it had been obvious from what they hadn't said that she would never live up to her parents' memories of the child they had lost.

The harder she'd tried, it seemed the more she'd failed, and when their disappointment had started to feel like knife thrusts she had decided to stop trying—it was just too bloody painful.

It had been about that time when Leo had entered her life and, for the first time in her life, she had not felt second best.

'Have I said something amusing?'

A look of confusion crossed her face as she dragged herself back to the present. 'What do you mean?'

'You laughed.' If you could call the strangled sound that had left her lips a laugh.

'Tickle,' she said, touching her throat, not quite meeting his eyes as she produced a very unrealistic cough behind her hand.

'The butter, it's just in there,' she said as he turned to the fridge door. 'That's right, second shelf,' she said, indicating the prettily decorated butter pats lined up. 'The one on the right is black garlic and that one is beef, both gorgeous.'

She was happy thinking about food. Food had always been a way to express herself—the tastes, the textures, the combination of spices, the routines—it had been her salvation because it all made perfect sense to her.

She blinked and fought the strong urge to close her eyes as she watched him methodically select the items he wanted and place them on a scrubbed wooden board, which he dumped on the freshly scrubbed copper surface beside her.

'What are you doing, Leo?' she protested wearily as she fought off the impulse to close her eyes. 'I've just cleaned this.'

'I am feeding you because you are clearly too stupid to feed yourself.'

'I'm not hungry.' But actually, she realised, she was ravenous.

She blinked and opened her eyes wide at the sound of him slicing into the loaf. She pinched herself to stay awake, or maybe she actually wasn't awake and this was all some bizarre nightmare as she watched him putting a generous slice on a plate and push it towards her. 'Eat.'

Dry bread was his version of food? It was funny, but her depleted energy levels didn't even allow for a smile, let alone a mocking laugh. 'You…?'

'I have eaten plenty.'

'Why are you being nice?' He had glanced at her but was busy dolloping some butter on the bread, along with a generous helping of the paté. 'You didn't bring me here to be nice.'

She took a bite, and felt her energy levels surge.

'So why do you think I brought you here?' He stepped back and watched her devour the food the way she had once devoured him.

'To rub my nose in it by showing me the life that could have been mine.' She wiped the crumbs from around her mouth. 'A bit obvious, but probably part of it is also about…control? You have it and I don't.' If this was what they called *speaking truth to power* she couldn't understand why it wasn't more popular. It felt great, also scarily addictive.

'Or maybe you wanted to see me overcome with lust?' Her eyes dropped, her scornful laugh sounding forced as she added quickly, 'Anyway, this—' her over-the-top gesture encompassed their surroundings '—is all a bit of an overkill. You didn't have to bring me here to prove you are some sort of irresistible sex god; you could have done that in London.'

One corner of his mouth lifted in a wicked smile and he watched the horrified panic spread across her face as she realised what she'd just said.

'Now she tells me,' he drawled, enjoying every moment of her discomfiture, not that she was telling him anything he didn't already know.

Amy might have changed but she still couldn't hide her physical response to him; he knew for a fact if he laid his hand against her breast he would be able to feel her heart trying to pound its way to freedom.

'I was just thinking of all those wasted air miles,' she bluffed. 'For the record, it doesn't matter what the location is, *nothing* is going to happen between us.'

'Was that declaration for your benefit or mine?'

Her nostrils flared as she glared. 'Your problem is—' She stopped the flow of words to give her brain time to catch up with her tongue by the simple expedient of biting down hard.

'Don't stop now; this is fascinating.'

A fresh wave of angry colour flooded her face. 'You know exactly what I meant,' she countered crossly.

'I think I do, yes.'

'Not that,' she snarled, longing to wipe the self-satisfied smirk off his face. 'Your problem is you've had too many casual hook-ups telling you how perfect you are because they know they'll never have to look at you with crumbs around your mouth.' Even as she spoke, her eyes zeroed in on the perfectly carved outline of his mouth, which was a mistake.

She cleared her throat. 'Seriously, although I'd love to pander to your ego with some more foot-in-mouth moments, it's been a long day and I've had enough,' she added, sliding the plate away.

'You've barely eaten anything, except me with your eyes.'

His silky taunt brought home the fact she was still staring at his mouth. 'Probably why I have indigestion.'

Her spiky riposte drew a laugh from his throat and an appreciative gleam to his eyes.

'Eat!' He slid the plate back to her.

'I'm sure that wasn't in the contract,' she grumbled, loading another slice of bread with butter and paté and taking a bite of a tomato before addressing the bread. 'I can feel my arteries clogging.'

Curious, Leo sampled the paté from a knife, belatedly aware that she was staring at his mouth again.

Amy lowered her eyes, admitting in a grudging mumble, 'I was hungry. I did need food, but it's hard when you're cooking to actually eat properly, especially when you finish late at night.'

He watched her lick some butter off her lips and angled his head, lowering his eyelids to hide the predatory gleam he couldn't prevent. Then he wondered why he was even bothering to hide anything when there was nothing covert about the electricity in the air or the hunger clawing at his gut.

He laid the knife down. 'It's good.'

She tipped her head in acknowledgment of the compliment and looked at him through her lashes. 'I went a bit heavy on the brandy.'

'Ever the critic.'

'I'm not into false modesty.'

'So you usually fall into bed after service.' *Alone?* he wondered, his eyes sliding of their own volition to the third—yes, he had been counting—button that had popped open at the neck of her blouse.

'That would be nice,' she admitted, directing her gaze away from the satiny gleam of the dark olive skin of his throat and at the rack of copper pans hanging on the stone wall instead. 'But it's hard to switch off after a busy service. Not that tonight was particularly busy. I've never worked in a kitchen so *over*staffed before.'

'So you like to keep busy?'

His words brought her eyes back to his face and, captured by his ink-black gaze, Amy couldn't have looked away if her life depended on it.

Why try? asked the unhelpful voice in her head. *He is extremely good to look at.*

She gave a twisted smile. 'When I'm not laundering money or entertaining my shady business partners, of course.'

He huffed out an impatient sigh. 'Don't be so damned prickly. But now we're on the subject, you do know that he was using you, that the bastard would have let you take the fall for him.'

Tears stung her eyelids as she nodded.

'Then why? Why the hell would you let him get away with it? Why let yourself be used that way?'

The muscles of Leo's face were clenched, pulled taut against his perfect bones. His sensual lips were compressed flat, almost bloodless as his nostrils flared, making her think of a jungle cat about to rip its prey apart.

'Can't you see he preys on your weakness?'

'I'm not weak. Caring about someone isn't weakness.' Her empty plate scraped along the gleaming copper surface as she pushed it away before pressing her hands, sweaty palms down, to lever herself off the surface and jump to the floor.

CHAPTER SIX

HER ATTITUDE INFURIATED him beyond reason. 'Care? Your father used you, screwed you over, and you are still putting your life on hold for him.' He pointed out the basic facts in what was intended to be an expressionless monotone but the anger he struggled to contain seeped like acid into his voice. 'You think that is a badge of courage? *Dio...!* It is stupid! And what sort of message does that send out? Here's my other cheek!' he snarled, turning his head to one side and poking a finger at his own lean cheek.

Amy was seized with a compulsion to reach out and lay her hand against his brown cheek, feel the stubble under her fingertips. She was unable to take her eyes off his face, all the passion in him drawing her like a moth to a flame.

'What are you staring at?'

'You are so Italian here.'

'It's not about geography; I am half Italian everywhere.'

'Well, you have certainly embraced the Latin thing.'

'Do not change the subject, Amy.'

'I'm not, I'm… Well, maybe just a little bit,' she conceded. 'My father—' she sighed out, dodging his accusing stare. 'He is my father; you must understand that, for all his faults. Your own grandfather—'

'Rejected my mother.' He enunciated each word slowly, the heat that had been in his voice becoming an icy coldness as he related his past. 'I barely remember, but she came from here. Imagine what it must have been like to go from this to the life she had. Her own father sent her into a life of penury and back-breaking misery. She was a single mother with nothing and…' He paused, the muscles in his throat working as he swallowed, visibly gaining control of his emotions as he finished in a voice now devoid of all emotion. 'Forgiveness does not come as easily to me as it appears to for you.'

'You have forgiven your grandfather, though.'

'I have *accepted* who he is; it is not quite the same thing.'

'After Mum died and then Dad was arrested and bailed…' she said slowly.

Some of the heat died from his face. 'Your mother always seemed like a nice person.'

She nodded, tears crowding her eyes. 'She was, but I think when Alice died… Losing a baby, a child, like that, it has to change you.' Hand on her throat, her chest lifted in a shuddering sigh. 'I always wish I had told her—'

He watched as she stopped, a stricken self-conscious expression, quickly banished, flashing across her face.

'Told her what?'

'Dad was devastated by her death and then… I was furious with him after the arrest, you know, especially after the police rolled up at Mum's funeral. We had massive rows and for the first time in years, I went to the stables. I even got on a horse.' She vented a hard little laugh at the memory. 'Just to punish him.'

'Did you enjoy it?'

The question made her smile wryly. 'I do love horses, but it turns out I'm not too good with heights.'

Her attempt to laugh at herself brought an ache to his throat. Leo was fully aware of the irony of his reaction. He had brought her here to punish her and he had fallen into the trap of wanting to protect her, but it was an impulse he had no intention of surrendering to. 'It is hardly surprising you were so angry with him.'

'I know, but...one night I came home. He'd been bailed awaiting sentencing the next day, but I still went out and left him. When I walked in there were empty pill bottles everywhere, and he was unconscious...'

The shock of her stark description nailed him to the spot. 'Your father attempted to take his own life?'

She nodded. 'It was lucky I came home when I did.'

Leo compressed his lips. Expressing his suspicions was not going to make anyone feel better, but he had to wonder, knowing the man as he did, if Sinclair had not very carefully timed his suicide attempt. Whatever the truth was, Amy being her father's protector now made much more sense.

'I don't know why I told you that.' Amy's smooth brow pleated as her eyes lifted to his face. It was stupid, considering he had appointed himself as her enemy, but she felt a sense of relief in finally having shared it.

Her legs felt shaky and she just hoped they would hold her up. During the to-and-fro of their conversation, a heat and a heavy raw awareness had been building until she could almost see and feel the blue crackle in the air, and not just in her legs.

'You've not eaten enough to keep a sparrow alive.' His voice was a sexy, dark silk rumble as he pre-empted her intention to move away by coming to stand in front of her, effectively pinning her with her back to the counter.

'I've had enough. I was breaking more health and safety rules than you can dream of by sitting on the work surface,' she said, her voice sounding a little high-pitched.

'I never dream of health and safety rules. Do you want to know what I dream about, Amy?'

Playing for time, she tucked stray strands of toffee-coloured hair behind her ears. The delay didn't help as when she opened her mouth a squeak came out. Not that Amy heard it past the mindless clamour in her blood—a driving desire to touch him becoming so loud it drowned out everything else. A bomb could have exploded and she wouldn't have heard it.

Her head lifted, her eyes half-closed, she could see the dark shadow of him through the delicate membrane.

'Your mouth.'

She blinked her eyes open to see that Leo was staring at the mouth he'd just mentioned.

'I dream about your laugh too…full-throated and the sexiest sound in the world.'

She gave a laugh now but it was nervous and breath-less, more a sigh than a laugh.

'I dream—'

Unable to stand further revelations, she cut across him. 'Not of revenge?'

Her words hit him like a bucket of ice water.

The sexual tension moved below critical point as he acknowledged the charge with a careless shrug.

'Another day, maybe? Right now, I want…' He leaned in and touched her cheek with his thumb, running down the soft curve until it came to rest at the side of her mouth before moving to the curved seal of her lips. 'I would like to explore every moist, warm crevice.'

Amy's lips parted on a gasp as his mouth replaced his thumb. The kiss was feather-soft.

Her world seemed to otherwise stop as their eyes met and he kissed her for real, hard and hungry, driving her head back against the support of his hand.

The heat was instantaneous, as was her loss of control, and Amy was on a high as liquid warmth spilled between her legs.

It was that familiar, often dreamt of growling sound that vibrated in her throat that made him pull back. It was either that or obey every raw instinct that was urging him to sink into her, take her right here on the damned kitchen floor.

She deserved better than that.

For a man out for revenge, Leo, you're showing way too much consideration, mocked the voice in his head.

'That felt like revenge.'

He looked stunned by her response.

'It was a kiss.' His shrug dismissed it as nothing.

It was calculated, it was Leo exploiting her weakness, her desire for him, and when she compared it to the kisses they had once shared, kisses filled with lust, love, laughter and tenderness, she wanted to weep for what she had lost.

She brushed the back of her hand across her trembling

lips as though to wipe away the touch and saw his eyes flare hot with some sort of emotion she didn't have the energy or inclination to translate.

Blinking, she stalked over to the row of sinks and picked up a cloth.

'What are you doing now?'

'I'm cleaning up the mess you've made.' The real *mess,* the tangle of conflicting emotions in her head, was not so easily dealt with, not with a wet cloth anyhow.

Maybe a bit of self-control required here, Amy.

The cloth was plucked from her hand and flung into a sink.

'Are you *trying* to be a martyr? You've been up since dawn and you've seen nothing but the kitchen—'

She gave an indignant gasp. The cheek of the man! 'And whose fault is that? You brought me in by the servants' entrance.'

His grimace was not guilt exactly, but something that came as close as she had ever seen or was likely to on his face, and a moment later it was gone.

'No one expected you to go straight to work.'

She fixed him with a narrow-eyed glare. 'What did you expect, Leo?'

Good question. 'Not what happened. Come on, I'll show you to your room.'

She curled her lips into a sarcastic smile. 'A cosy cellar somewhere, I can't wait.'

'I think we can at least manage hot and cold running water.' He caught her gaze moving to the work surface and the plate and his lips tightened. 'Leave it; someone else will attend to it.'

'My, you really have grown into the arrogant billionaire lifestyle, haven't you, Leo? I *am* the someone else that does the attending,' she muttered, but her heart wasn't in it. Weariness was washing over her as the day's events finally caught up with her.

His eyes had narrowed but as he studied her face he simply shrugged. 'I'll give you the grand tour tomorrow, but we'll use the shortcut tonight.'

She hadn't noticed the stone spiral staircase in the lobby when they had arrived.

She was too tired to argue, too strung out on the emotions he'd dragged out of her, from the depths of her past.

By the time she had followed him to the top she had stopped counting the floors they had passed and was breathing hard.

'This is the direct route from the service section to the east tower wing.'

Amy pictured the castle as she had arrived, the square twin towers that had loomed over the iconic edifice. 'So we're in the tower now?'

'Yes, both towers, along with the defensive wall, were here before the rest came along in the mid-fourteenth century. They are no longer separate but part of the house itself.'

'Your family have lived here all that time?'

'We came along in the fifteenth century.'

'Almost newbies then.'

He might have smiled at her quip but he was too far ahead to tell and she was almost skipping to keep up.

'The castle transformed over the years into a fortified mansion rather than a castle; there is one floor above us.'

'How many floors are there?'

'Seven. This floor links with the wing above the library.'

She blinked, finding it impossible to visualise the layout. 'It looked pretty much like a castle to me. Do the other staff have accommodation here?' she said, lowering her voice as they walked down a wide, shallow flight of stairs and entered a hallway. They passed by several doors. A few of the deep windows to her right were open and she could hear the sound of the sea, her nose twitching as she inhaled the salty tang in the warm breeze that was underlaid with the mingled scents of cypress and thyme.

'There are converted outbuildings, stable blocks,' he explained, not slowing his stride. 'But most live in the village, a few commute from town.'

Her weariness outweighed her curiosity so she resisted the temptation to ask for more details, but decided that she would find out about the village as it would mean less interaction with Leo. Because after that scene in the kitchen, which she had barely escaped with her mind intact, it was clear that even a distant glimpse of him was not going to be good for her equilibrium. Though she was clinging to the very realistic hope that he wouldn't be here often.

Wanting to plaster herself against him while simultaneously wanting to push him away was making her head ache. Just looking at him made the rest of her ache. His antagonism hurt, but the small snatches of conversation that came close to the easy intimacy they had once shared were even more painful reminders of what she'd lost.

She half tripped, steadied herself and bit her lip, determined not to ask him to slow down even though she was virtually skipping now to keep up with his long stride. A more considerate man might have made allowances for the disparity in their leg lengths, she decided, nursing her resentment.

'Here we are.'

He had stopped outside a double door, the only door in this section of the hallway that she could see. With any luck, this meant she would be less likely to bump into any guests; she already knew that twenty were staying the night after the dinner.

'Thanks.' She stood, waiting for him to move. 'I just hope I will be able to find my way to the kitchen in the morning.' She kept the doubt out of her voice to keep things light.

'You won't be needed in the kitchen in the morning.' He watched her stick her little rounded chin out and sighed. The image he carried of a soft helpless creature who needed someone to make her decisions for her was fast vanishing.

Who was he kidding? It had already gone, and he was feeling quite nostalgic for it. Despising her had made it easier to keep any lingering sexual attraction that remained from their youthful fling at bay.

Obviously, Leo no longer mistook the high voltage sparks that flew between them for love. The wild hunger they both still felt might be nothing more than chemistry, but it was still an obstacle—certainly to a good night's sleep. But it went both ways, and he had no qualms about using it against her—using it to his own advantage.

'I will be needed.'

His jaw clenched and her expression suggested she took pleasure from contradicting him.

'It's *breakfast!* I am sure the rest of the army down there can cope without your guidance.'

'Do I tell you how to do…whatever it is you do? The morning isn't just breakfast, it's deliveries and menus and prep,' she enumerated, mocking his ignorance.

Though it turned out he wasn't as clueless as she had imagined when he said, 'Deliveries aren't really an issue as almost everything is produced in-house, so to speak. You can literally walk around the kitchen gardens and select your fresh produce. Our herds are all organic free range, and even most of the wine is produced here, or it will be. You asked what I do, and the winery is my pet project at the moment.'

She looked impressed, which gave him a feeling of smug satisfaction.

'And *your* morning will involve meeting my grandfather,' he added, pausing to watch her eyes widen in predictable shock, probably dismay too.

If she knew his grandfather it would definitely be dismay. He could have made an excuse when the old man had announced he wanted to meet this new chef and possibly steal her from Leo, on whom good food was wasted, but Leo had decided that the demand fitted well into his plan to make Amy's life uncomfortable.

So far, he'd not had the success he had anticipated in that regard; he'd been overconfident. Amy had responded to every challenge and the kiss that should have unsettled her hadn't done so either!

'But…'

He cut across her wavering protest. 'A courtesy, just to say hello. He was really impressed with the food tonight.'

'Does he not live here?'

'No, he stepped aside from the day-to-day running a few years ago. He currently lives in Florence, so now I'm the one paying your wages.'

'How much?'

A raw laugh was wrenched from his throat. 'You didn't read that page?'

'I didn't see much point. This is blackmail, not a job, so I didn't think I could really negotiate my salary.'

His head reared back, an expression of hauteur spreading across his lean face.

'You're *offended?*' she cried incredulously. 'Sorry, but it's the truth! If you must know, I hadn't thought about it; you're paying the salary of my replacement at the food truck, so I assumed...'

'What, that you could just sit back, whip up an omelette and wait for this to be over? You will earn your pay.'

Outraged at the suggestion that she wouldn't, her golden-brown eyes sparked. 'I am *not* work-shy.'

'I had noticed that.'

His dry response mollified her slightly. 'So when is this *audience* with your grandfather?' As much as she disliked the idea, she couldn't see any way around it.

His expressive lips quirked at her choice of words. 'We should be able to do the tour first.'

'*We?*' she said warily.

'I will give you the tour, then introduce you to my grandfather.'

'I could wander around on my own—'

'And get lost.'

'I happen to have an excellent sense of direction,' she

lied. 'But fine, I'll do the tour. Go for it, show me all the things I missed out on, rub my nose in it…'

'What the hell are you talking about?'

She raised one well-defined brow. 'Oh, come off it, Leo. I may be dim enough to let Dad dupe me, but I'm not that dim. This is obviously part of your payback; you want to show me the life that could have been mine, had I stayed with you. The thing is, even if I had gone with you, we likely wouldn't be together now. Have you seen the statistics on young marriage?'

'I don't recall ever proposing.'

Swallowing the urge to weep because he'd probably like it if she did, she shrugged. 'True, we weren't that foolish, but you know what I mean.'

As he finally stepped aside, Amy virtually threw herself into the room but, before she could close the door on him, he brushed past her and went inside. She took a deep breath and turned slowly to face him.

'I don't need a guided tour of my room—' She stopped mid-sentence, her stunned gaze moving around the room, even though her initial thought was that it was a mistake.

This was not a bedroom, but a sitting room. A further internal door was open and she could make out an elegant antique pale wooden half tester bed hung with pretty drapes.

This room had a feminine vibe too, the furniture a blend of antique and high-end modern. The pale linen upholstery on the comfortable-looking sofas was brightened by an eclectic selection of cushions. Similarly, the rugs on the polished wooden floor provided vivid splashes of colour, as did the antique rugs, probably too precious to walk on, glowing against the stone walls. She tracked the gorgeous scent that filled the room to the antique bowl set in the carved open fireplace that held lavender and roses.

She hadn't been expecting…this.

'This is beautiful,' she said, wandering across the polished boards of the floor to the open doorway of the bedroom, her expression one of genuine pleasure.

'Right, so you were thinking more a dusty attic and slave labour; that explains your decision to spend half the night outside the door picking a fight with me.'

'I was not picking a fight. I was *winning* a fight.' She paused. Actually, they had been talking; she had not expected that being here would involve so much talking. 'And, besides, you were…'

'I was?' he prompted.

'It doesn't matter.' She had no intention of explaining that because entering the room involved physical contact with him, it had not been an option. They were not touching and the heat rising from the pit of her belly was already shamefully distracting.

He was watching her with an uncomfortably alert expression in his midnight inky stare. When he spoke it was slowly, a discernible edginess in his deep velvet voice.

'We could always just do it instead of skating around it; just cut to the chase and get it over with.' He took a step towards her and Amy, engulfed by a wave of sheer panic, mirrored the action, two steps to his one, which took her into the bedroom.

'Get what over with?' Her attempt at bewilderment drew an impatient shake of his head and an eye roll.

'Don't pretend you don't know what I'm talking about, Amy. Neither of us are starry-eyed kids any more, calling sex *love*.'

She stood there, her insides molten, her mind floating somewhere outside her body.

He watched as she bit down on her full upper lip, the soft cushiony pinkness taunting him. Her hurried shallow breaths and dilated pupils sending messages that were louder than words.

He could almost hear his control snapping. He moved and at the last second from somewhere he dug out the strength to control the desire that was pounding at him.

'You've got to stop looking at me like that if you don't want this to happen, Amy.'

Amy couldn't have broken free of his hypnotic stare if her life had depended on it. Moreover, she didn't want to.

'It is true, I do want sex…with you.' His inner tension added a sexy rasp to his voice. 'Are you trying to tell me you don't want it too?'

She met his hypnotic gaze and said nothing. The only sound in the room was the distant ticking of a clock and the audible breathy rasp of her forced respirations.

'I… You…' She shook her head, *needing* to touch him so much it was a physical pain.

He could see her shaking and had to forcibly stop himself from reaching for her. Knowing a woman wanted you was an aphrodisiac; knowing *this* woman in particular wanted him was an incredible rush.

'I need to hear you say it. If you want me, *cara,* come and get me!' Sweat dampened his skin as he threw out the challenge whilst ruthlessly checking the painful need rising up in him.

Nine years ago, she had sent him away, so it was important, *essential,* to him that this time she be the one begging him to stay.

She counted the steps as she maintained contact with the molten heat of his stare, only stopping when there was barely an inch of air separating them. The heat coming off his body made it feel like a furnace.

'I want you.'

The heat burst white-hot around them as their lips connected.

He groaned as she slid her tongue sinuously between his lips and, framing her face between his hands, he plunged deeper into the warm, moist recesses of her mouth.

Her breasts flattened against his rock-hard chest as she strained against him, drawing herself up on tiptoe to link her fingers behind his head.

Desire burned away everything in her head but Leo. They stumbled backwards, lips still connected, to the bed and fell down together onto it.

Leo rolled onto his side, bringing her with him, before he stood up, drawing a cry of loss and protest from Amy until she saw he was fighting his way out of his shirt.

She pulled herself up onto her knees to watch him, taking gloating pleasure from eyeing his lean tanned torso, from the perfect musculature of his broad chest down to the ridges corrugating his flat belly.

His burning eyes left hers to deal with his belt buckle. 'You carry on looking at me like that and things might be over before they've even begun,' he purred, the molten heat in his stare stoking the fire inside her.

'You're shaking,' she pushed out, consumed by an ever-escalating sense of urgency. 'Let me,' she demanded fiercely.

The blood burning in his veins, Leo sank his fingers

into her hair as, head bent, she worked on the buckle before she moved to the zip. Swiftly, he caught her hands, holding them wide.

Unable to resist her sultry smile, he bent down, kissing her while he opened her shirt by the simple expedient of pulling hard, sending a shower of buttons across the room as he peeled the fabric off her shoulders. She fell back on her bottom and had wriggled her jeans over her slim hips in a matter of moments.

The man who women generally considered a slick, polished lover fumbled to strip off his own trousers, but this was no sex by numbers; it was raw and elemental, no rules, just anger and need. He had never wanted a woman this much in his life.

Amy gasped as his mouth trailed heat and moisture over her bare shoulder and neck as he joined her on the bed. Head flung back, she linked her arms around his waist as he freed her breasts from her bra and turned his attention to the quivering peaks, cupping, stroking, kneading as she arched her back to give him full access.

Pausing for a moment, he removed his boxer shorts, allowing his erection to fall straight into her waiting greedy hands, and they closed over the shaft, drawing a deep feral groan from the depths of his chest.

He returned to pay homage to her breasts once more, his tongue flicking a taut nipple. As need pounded through him, Leo fought for some sort of control when all he wanted to do was plunge straight into her softness.

'You're beautiful,' he rasped as he removed the tiny panties she wore and propped himself up on one elbow to stare down at her now totally nude body.

She took his hand and guided it to the apex of her

legs and the soft fuzz there. Her eyes drifted closed as he began to stroke her.

Her body was ready for him before he even touched her, so wet and hot as his fingers slid over the intimate folds.

Throbbing with need, he kissed his way up her body before sliding between her open legs. Her back arched as he rotated his hips before sliding incrementally deeper inside her, and she closed around him, tight as a glove.

As they moved together seamlessly, Leo felt the loneliness he never acknowledged melt away in the heat of their union, the softness of her body, the total surrender she offered him.

As the firestorm of sensation built inside her, Amy not only forgot how to breathe, she forgot where she ended and Leo began. It was a total immersion in a perfect, decadent storm of ecstasy that only ended when it finally exploded and annihilated them both.

Lying there, breathing hard, stunned by the intensity of the moment, she felt him kiss her eyelids and couldn't help a nip of fear. She was affected too much by what had just happened.

Confused by the flurry of movement from Leo, Amy opened her eyes and watched him, at first bewildered and then understanding, as she realised there would be no intimate aftermath.

'You're going?' she said, keeping her voice carefully neutral as she pulled the sheet up over her cooling body.

Retrieving his shirt from where it had fallen, his eyes brushed her face and, ignoring the hand squeezing his heart, he nodded. He had to keep moving because he hadn't wanted to leave the bed at all; he had wanted to stay there and hold her.

That should not happen when you scratched a carnal itch, he thought, and it was a relief to recognise the loneliness he usually wore like armour settle firmly back into place. As he dressed, he welcomed the return of the hollow ache inside that was a permanent part of him.

'Get some sleep, Amy. I'll see you in the morning,' he called over his shoulder before he left the room, closing the door behind him.

She heard the door slam but didn't see his exit because she had turned over and was pummelling the pillows with her fists as mortification rolled over her in waves.

She really hated him for doing that to her.

She wasn't too keen on herself either right now, for being such a total pushover.

Outside in the hallway, Leo leaned his shoulders against the wall and thrust his long fingers into his hair. Tilting his head back, he gently banged it against the wall, the sinews in his neck standing out like cords under his olive skin.

He stood there for several moments until his erratic breathing slowed and became regular again. He was in danger of complicating things, and he refused to do that. They shared a natural chemistry, that was all. Yes, it was hot, but it would inevitably cool, and so the sane thing to do would be to enjoy it while it lasted. Some heavy-duty sexual release would be both curative and pleasurable. It would wipe the slate and his head clean of the lingering chaos Amy had left behind.

It should have been a cut and dried deal. Logically, it would have been, had she not changed. He'd been deeply invested in her being the same sweet, pliable and ultimately weak Amy he'd known her to be.

He'd needed her to be *that* Amy.

His teeth gritted in a frustrated grimace. Instead, she was *this* Amy.

The one who had stepped outside the box he had put her in and then crushed it under her small heel.

The one who stood up to him, who was not anxious in the slightest to please.

And the hell of it was, he found this new Amy even more attractive.

He shook his head, the groove between his brows deepening as he relived the staggering moment that peace had broken out when she'd stepped into a kitchen of warring egos, without even raising her voice.

She had managed them and they didn't even know they were being managed. Was there a fear that she would manage him too, if he let her?

CHAPTER SEVEN

THE LAST TIME Amy had glanced at the clock it had been four a.m. As she reached for her phone and glanced blearily at the screen, she saw it was now half-past seven. She lifted a hand to shade her eyes from the light that was shining through the window as she hadn't drawn the blinds last night.

Carefully, she pushed off the covers and tentatively swung her legs over the edge of the bed. Her head was pounding like a metronome. The events of yesterday, especially the last part, flickered through her head in slow motion. The way her body had become so quickly attuned to his again, the realisation that she had wanted him so badly, frightened her.

Even though she still wanted him.

She opened one eye. Had she packed her migraine medication? She already knew the answer was no, but screaming would have hurt and escalated the issue, so instead she walked across to the window and searched for the mechanism that closed the blinds.

The relief when the sun was blotted out drew a deep sigh from her. Locating her handbag, she found the strip of generic painkillers which would be a lot better than nothing, especially if they kicked in before the migraine developed claws and took hold.

She lay back down on the bed and waited for the meds to kick in; she knew how this worked. Half an hour later, she tested the water by sitting up. The fact that she could, without feeling dizzy or wanting to throw up, suggested the painkillers had done their job, which was a massive relief. Whatever else Leo had in store for her today, meeting his grandfather, who did not sound warm and cuddly, would require her to be on her A game.

A fuzziness persisted but she was able to open a selection of doors revealing generous storage without wincing when they closed. She finally located the door that led to the bathroom, which turned out to be enormous, bigger than her entire flat in London. So big she could have lived in it. Even in her downbeat mood she paused to lust a little over the incredible copper bath.

This was her fantasy and Leo's real life.

They had no future together. He had everything he wanted at his fingertips...*including her.* And when he didn't, when the spark fizzled out, she thought of all those years of crushing loneliness she had fought her way free of. What had she been thinking, opening the door to it happening all over again?

That it had been a mistake hardly covered it, and yet she knew that if she could live last night again, she'd do exactly the same thing.

Eyes closed, she walked into the shower. The water wasn't cold but it did drown out the condemnatory voice in her head.

She spent an age standing under the steamy jets of the walk-in shower with the space-age controls, being pounded from all sides. It was hedonistic. How long was it since she had lingered like this in a shower? A smile curved her lips as she enjoyed the self-indulgent luxury of it. She enjoyed the luxury too of wrapping herself in one of the stack of fluffy bath sheets, until she realised she didn't have a clue what time it was.

Amy was stunned; she *always* knew what time it was. Her life revolved around being at work on time and working systematically through the long list of tasks she needed to complete. That was how she made it through each day. She could never let up because if she did her life would immediately spin out of control.

And her real fear, the one she didn't acknowledge, was that *she* would also spin out of control.

She shook her head and immediately regretted the action. Too many people had expected—still expected—too much from her for that to happen. Even when she'd lost Leo, she hadn't allowed herself the opportunity to break down, to let go. She'd hassled the hurt away.

In search of her phone, she squatted down and went through the pockets of the clothes she had just dropped in a messy pile on the floor when she had stripped off last night.

It had fallen out of a pocket and it was low on charge but intact. When she saw the time, she gave a worried frown.

What if Leo appeared?

And how was she going to play the morning after the night before?

Or maybe after last night he wouldn't want to see her, she speculated, worrying when she recognised the thought was not as cheering as it might be—*should* be.

She took one of the robes that were hanging on a rack, then wrapped a towel turban-wise around her dripping hair. Tying the belt on the robe, she hurried through into the adjoining room as she worked out her coping strategy for dealing with him. For starters, she was going to turn it into a drama.

There was no sign of her suitcase.

After a lot of searching, she discovered her case and her clothes behind the last door she opened. Her clothes were all neatly hung up and folded.

Half an hour later, fully dressed and her hair almost dry, the damp braid hanging down between her shoulder blades, she had returned to the bathroom to retrieve her clothes when there was a knock that appeared to be coming from the direction of the outer door. She froze, listening, then heard a female voice call something she could not make out and a moment later she heard the door quietly close again.

Some of the tension left her shoulders; at least it wasn't Leo. Ignoring the anticlimactic feeling this realisation brought with it, she checked herself out in the mirror. She was now as pink as she had just been pale. Scowling at the reflected face of the person who stared back at her, she thrust her clothes into a linen hamper and, taking a deep breath, opened the door.

The bedroom was empty, and so was the pretty sunlit sitting room. She blinked in the sunlight and squinted, shading her eyes with a hand. The person who had entered before had opened a window and delivered the tray responsible for the gorgeous aroma of coffee.

In deference to her fragile head, she half-lowered the

blinds and eagerly followed the scent to the table where the tray and coffee pot sat.

Did staff get coffee delivered to their rooms?

Did they have rooms like this?

Or only the ones who slept with the boss?

The attention, while very nice, made it hard to gauge her position on the upstairs-downstairs gradient. It was going to be hard to establish a working relationship with the other kitchen staff if they thought she was getting preferential treatment.

Or sleeping with the boss.

Was this about Leo not losing an opportunity to drive home what he now had, and she didn't? The best response to him trying to make her feel uncomfortable was to enjoy the perks, she decided. So she poured herself a cup and sipped contentedly as she took the time to examine her surroundings in a little more detail.

The first thing that caught her eye was a small button on the floor by the open bedroom door. Remembering how it had got there sent a hungry hormonal rush through her body.

She had decided to put down her behaviour last night to a combination of serious exhaustion and the fact that her sexual appetite had been virtually in hibernation for the past nine years.

It had taken Leo to reawaken it.

The thought sent a bolt of sheer panic through her as, with perfect timing, the door opened, not preceded by a knock, polite or otherwise.

Leo stood framed there for a moment, the image of his tall figure managing to imprint itself on her retinas.

His nostrils flared as his glance was drawn to the tray. 'Is there a spare cup?'

She delivered a sweet smile before looking at him and, when she did, it stayed pasted there. She cleared her throat.

'There is. Anyone would think someone knew you were coming when they ordered it.' She had decided that if he mentioned last night she would just shrug and be cool, maybe even slightly amused that he was making a big deal out of nothing.

He hadn't mentioned last night yet; he hadn't done anything except send her pulse into orbit.

In her defence, he would do that to anyone, rocking up without warning in track bottoms and a damned running vest that clung damply to his golden skin which, gleaming against the black fabric, oozed pheromones from every perfect pore.

She fiddled with her hair as she tried and failed to look anywhere but at him.

'Sorry, I ran for longer than I intended.'

She pressed her fingers to her temple, but she had no intention of telling him about her migraine, revealing any weakness.

'Sorry as well about…' His gesture took in his running outfit.

She licked her dry lips and swallowed, privately thinking that his smile was less apology and more taunt.

'I didn't want to keep you hanging around before we started the tour.' With a frown, he walked across to the first window and raised the blind, before performing the same action on the other two.

She was stubbornly unwilling to ask him to lower

them again. The discomfort was preferable to admitting a vulnerability to Leo. She adjusted her seat with her back to the windows and watched in silence as he poured his coffee.

He took a long swallow that caused the muscles in his throat to ripple before he folded himself casually into one of the armchairs. It wasn't really built for someone of his stature but he was incapable of doing anything that wasn't elegant and coordinated.

She practised a cool reply in her head but was fatally distracted. His body hummed with energy but underneath she could sense the tension vibrating off him.

Well, she reasoned waspishly, it only seemed right that the life of a billionaire should have some degree of stress. Maybe those articles she had read that claimed he slept the moment his head hit the pillow and woke up refreshed six hours later were part of the fictional narrative that surrounded him.

The women weren't fictional though.

She experienced a moment of stomach-clenching nausea that she refused point-blank to acknowledge as jealousy.

'I didn't think it was a firm—'

'Date?'

'*Arrangement*,' she inserted, her smile insincere but the accompanying scowl very authentic as she ignored the mocking note in his voice. 'Another day will do just as well and if you're busy it might be quite fun to explore on my own.' Actually, a pair of dark glasses and some fresh air might, with the help of the painkillers, see off the incipient migraine.

'It was firm, and I'm not in any hurry.' He turned

towards her as the light shifted and fell on her face, bleaching her skin of colour and emphasising the size and brilliance of her soft brown eyes. He frowned.

'Did you sleep OK?'

'Like a baby,' she lied cheerfully. 'Did you have a good run, or workout, or—' She swallowed as her eyes remained unwilling to stop following the progress of a bead of sweat that slid down his chest.

'There is a gym and a pool inside and out, so feel free to make use of them.' He had made full use of them both before his run. He had exhausted his body though not his mind, which had only eventually cleared as he had pounded the forest trail.

He was overthinking everything. There was no problem to work through; he was not a hormonal teenager, and neither was he one of those men who waxed lyrical about emotional connections.

Last night had been sex, pretty mind-blowing, excellent sex, to be sure, but just sex.

'I don't expect I'll have time,' she said, resurrecting a little defiance.

'Do you have an issue with what I'm wearing?' he drawled, setting his drained cup back on the tray.

Her lips pursed tight as she glared at him and thought, *Thanks for drawing attention to the fact I can't take my eyes off you.*

'I was just thinking that you're not looking very executive today.'

No, just sexily gorgeous.

And he knew it.

Swallowing, she forcibly removed her eyes from the

second bead of sweat that was tracing a slower path down the glistening skin of his throat.

Behind his half-closed, heavy lids she could see the gleam in his inky eyes and she tensed, preparing for another jibe. Only she was left stunned when instead he said, 'You look beautiful this morning. We never did get to spend a night together, did we?'

Despite her innocence, or for that matter his own, she had not been overendowed with inhibitions. In fact, Leo thought, she had usually taken a wicked delight in shocking him.

He'd had more skilful lovers since her, but not one of them had ever come close to living up to the youthful, carnal initiation they had shared.

Until last night, he had sometimes wondered if he was guilty of embroidering their fireworks in bed with nostalgia.

Now he knew he hadn't.

He watched her through his lashes, the angle of her jaw, her shell-like earlobe... *Dio*, what the hell was happening to him? He was getting aroused by a woman's jaw!

Everything she did was just so... He took a final gulp from the nearly empty cup and got to his feet, moving restlessly around the room. His research into her life would have revealed any long-term relationships, but he considered it impossible that a woman with her innate sensuality would have lived the life of a nun.

Still, the knowledge that she was OK with casual hook-ups did not totally erase the unease he felt about last night, but he shelved the idea of the faceless men who had passed through her life, not finding it a subject he wanted to dwell on. At the same time, he was well aware that, considering his own lifestyle, his disapproval of hers was incredibly hypocritical.

'Last night…'

'A mistake, I know.'

'Inevitable is what I was thinking.'

'Oh!' She folded her hands primly in her lap and lowered her gaze.

'I was… I mean I…don't always act with so little… finesse.'

She looked up and was astonished to see embarrassment flit across his face.

'You were perfect!'

Her blush amused him.

'So were you.'

'This could get complicated, Leo.'

'What are you agonising about? We're not in a relationship, so why should there be any complications?'

Not for him, maybe, because he didn't even like her, whereas she… 'I don't like the assumption that you consider me being here as your sex on tap. That really isn't in my contract, not even the small print.'

He looked astonished by her outburst before he laughed. 'Don't stress,' he said, studying her face. 'Let's play it by ear, shall we? For the record, I'm quite happy to be your sex on tap for the duration. You going to eat this?' he asked, lifting the cover on a croissant and putting it in his mouth before she replied.

'I don't eat breakfast.' It was a lie, but he didn't need to know that.

'You're eating me up instead.' Underneath the sly, mocking accusation there was a tell-tale layer of tension that communicated itself directly to her tingling nerve-endings. The prickling sensation spread like a hot rash under her skin.

The automatic denial died on her lips when she realised she was staring at his mouth. She yanked her gaze upwards, connecting with his eyes, but the expression in the dark glimmering depths provided no safe space from the debilitating awareness that permeated her body.

'With your eyes,' he elaborated, presumably just in case she hadn't got the drift.

'You do think a lot of yourself, but actually I was thinking you might have showered before you invited yourself in,' she said with a fastidious little sniff as she shoved her hand in her handbag and pulled out a pair of oversized sunglasses and slid them on her nose.

Her eyes hidden, her chin took the heavy lifting when it came to challenging him to comment.

His response demolished any illusion that she was in control of this situation.

'You have changed. You used not to have any issue with my sweat. Quite the opposite, in fact.'

Her nostrils flared as she remembered the taste and smell of his damp skin.

She cleared her throat and blinked away the tactile images crowding into her head as Leo levered himself out of the chair with stomach-flipping, casual grace and rubbed his hands together.

'So, shall we get this thing over with?'

'What over with?'

'The tour. What did you think I meant, *cara*?'

'Will you stop calling me that?' she snapped out irritably, hating the way his tongue curled around the endearment, dragging each syllable out.

'Why? I am Italian. It's natural for me to say it.'

She turned her head, trying to avoid the smell of the coffee in her nostrils, a fragrance she normally loved but the migraine messed with all her senses.

'Did you never realise that you had family here? Did your mother never speak of…? Sorry, I didn't mean to—' She hesitated, not sure she should ask, not sure she had the right.

'Poke your delightful little nose in?' He shrugged, his eyes detaching from her face.

Amy's shoulders sagged. She was relieved both to escape his scrutiny and not be called out for her curiosity.

'My mother…no, never.'

Amy had the feeling that his words were not really addressed to her. He was barely acknowledging her presence; it was almost as if he had forgotten she was there.

He was still speaking.

'At least until she got ill. At the very end, she was on strong medication and she did speak of this place, though I didn't know that then as she kept sliding into Italian.'

'It seems odd she didn't speak Italian to you growing up.'

His flickering regard landed back on her face. 'What is this, twenty questions?'

She expected him to end the conversation and was surprised when, after a pause, he disclosed some more.

'I think my mother was trying to erase her background. I did know a few words, actually, and some phrases she said sometimes. When she called out for her *papà*, I assumed he was dead. I carried on thinking that for a long time.'

'It's so sad, but it must have been marvellous to know you weren't alone,' she said softly.

He imagined her eyes behind the dark sunglasses glowing with an empathy that struck him as ironic in the circumstances.

'I had thought once before I wasn't alone, but it turned out I was mistaken.' He brought his white teeth together, his shark-like smile more like a grimace as he watched her pale and virtually ooze guilt. 'Don't look so worried, Amy. What doesn't kill you and all that. So, are you ready?'

'I just need my...' She flung the words over her shoulder as she quickly disappeared into the bathroom. She needed a minute. She had reached the point of no return on the tears that refused to be blinked away behind the misted tinted glass.

What was she crying about, anyway?

He was never going to forgive her, she knew that. For a long time she had struggled to forgive herself, but she knew that if she had to make the choice again, she still would. That didn't make it the right decision but, right or wrong, she had to live with it.

And she had been living with it, in a water-under-the-bridge, moving on kind of way, but now, being here, seeing Leo, and remembering who he had once been...

He had moved on and so had she. Their lives were briefly connecting again, that was all.

On that tear-drying, pragmatic thought she snatched a tissue, blew her nose and wiped the mist from her glasses with her sleeve and went to locate her trainers from where she must have kicked them off last night. If Leo wanted to give her a tour, he could give her a tour. Anything that got them out of this room was a bonus.

Leo had watched Amy leave the room, admiring the view. He was still struggling to keep his libido in check when she returned, still pale in the face and huffing out breaths as she balanced on the foot that was shoved in an unlaced trainer, while with her knee brought up almost to her chin she tried to put the other on.

'There's no fire. Sit down before you do yourself an injury,' he barked out roughly.

She obeyed, quite literally dropping to the floor and straight into a cross-legged position, where she proceeded to push her bare foot into the trainer before leaping to her feet again.

Had she always been like that? Always on the go, rushing around? There were certainly things that had changed. Her face was a little thinner, the youthful softness of her features had become more refined, her rounded cheeks more pronounced, her stubborn chin a little sharper.

But her figure seemed exactly the same as he remembered it.

An image from the many stored in his head surfaced unbidden through the wall he had erected to hold back what he had mentally filed as juvenile fantasies.

Except this fantasy had been real.

Amy, the rosy tips of her breasts showing through her silky hair as she bent over him, her hands either side of his head, her hair brushing his chest.

He fought free of the images that belonged to a time

in his life when he had actually wanted ties, a time when he had not understood the advantages of no obligation, uncomplicated, honest sex.

Being transfixed by the rise and fall of her breasts beneath the loose cotton covering was an expression of nothing more complicated than a physical need, no more meaningful than slaking a thirst.

Sure, think of her as a glass of beer, Leo, mocked his internal voice. *That's really going to work!*

Oblivious to the fact that Leo was fighting against memories, Amy was focused on coaxing her features into a neutral expression that didn't hint at the painful friction caused by her breasts pushing against the fabric of her white shirt while she trawled frantically for a response, because the truth was not an option.

'Let's get this over with. I have work to do.' Work was her salvation during tough times, all times really. When she was thinking of spice combinations, tastes and textures she could shut out the background noise—or at least turn down the volume.

He opened the door into the corridor she vaguely recalled from last night, and she really wished all her memories of last night were as vague.

She stepped past him, walking into the corridor in daylight giving the brief illusion that she was stepping into the sea and sky. When the illusion faded, she realised that there was solid ground under her feet and the sea was several hundred metres beyond the ten-foot-high windows. She lifted a hand to offer another level of protection from the bright sunlight.

'You're not a fan of delegation then?' he wondered, joining her.

Light spots dancing across her vision, she turned away from the vista that another time she would have enjoyed. Her retinas made Leo a dark, threatening shadow against the light.

'I don't ask anyone to do anything I can't. I've never been what anyone would term an *executive* chef. I'm hands-on, even when I was working at the restaurant,' she explained, throwing a glance at her small hands with the neatly trimmed pearly nails. 'We might not have kept the Michelin star, even if we hadn't closed. There's a lot of pressure to maintain it, and for me it was never about attracting an elitist custom base. I just wanted to serve good food that only the elite could afford.'

Leo followed the direction of her gaze. Other than last night, he hadn't seen those elegant fingers chopping and dicing, but he had plenty of first-hand experience of them stroking and touching his flesh, featherlight and skilful. His body hardened, helpless to resist the ache of hunger in his belly.

His teeth clenched as he told himself he wasn't helpless; he was fully in control of himself.

'Very egalitarian of you.'

She ignored his mockery. 'In my experience, throwing around orders isn't the quickest way to gain respect.' She felt her shoulders relax. They were not retracing their footsteps from the previous night and the windows framing the views had been replaced by stone sconces containing bas-relief figures carved in the niches. They looked intricate but not friendly.

'Do you need respect?'

'Well, it's handy, especially when there's a kitchen full of professionals way more experienced than I am.'

She had realised that when she'd recognised the names and a quick internet trawl on her phone had confirmed her suspicions; the level of experience in the Romano kitchen was staggering.

'They are being asked to perform at a level way below their pay grade, so it has to be frustrating. It explains the atmosphere last night when we walked in, and it wasn't just me being foisted on them.'

'Are chefs meant to be so self-deprecating? I thought arrogance came with the job.'

Her eyes widened a second before her lips began to twitch and she choked back a laugh. So ironic, considering the man who'd just said that oozed arrogance from every perfect pore!

'Share the joke?'

She opened her eyes behind the smoky glass, this time not trying to stifle her laughter. 'Oh, I doubt you'd get it if I did. I'm just impressed that *self-deprecating* is in your vocabulary. And, for the record, I'm not underselling myself. I'm good at what I do, but—'

'But nothing,' he interrupted, recovering from the novelty shock of being mocked. 'The reason those highly qualified people are working under you is because they accepted a lot of money to do so—I only employ the best of the best.'

His comment had confirmed what Amy had suspected. 'Too many leaders, too many egos. But none big enough to compete with yours, of course.' She paused, seeing they had reached a gallery. The hallway continued on to the right, almost to infinity, it seemed, and they stood directly at the head of a staircase.

Curving and graceful, it led down to a massive space.

On a raised dais at one end, a grand piano took pride of place, and the marble floor had a pearlescent quality warmed by the ancient vibrant frescoes on the walls.

Amy blinked, the breath catching in her throat as she imagined what the room would look like when the chandeliers suspended from the coffered ceiling high above were lit, illuminating the intricately carved supporting pillars and bas-relief sculptures.

'The ballroom.'

She shot a self-conscious sideways look at his dark profile and closed her mouth with an audible snap. Though, in her defence, if ever a space deserved open-mouthed admiration this was it. Then, unable to resist the impulse, she ran her hand across the smooth inlaid wood of the curving bannister, enjoying the tactile sensation.

'What's the scent?' Finally, something that wasn't making her feel nauseous.

'Cedarwood.'

'I can imagine people making quite an entrance down this staircase,' she said, tilting her head back to look at the frescoes above and immediately regretting it when a sharp pain stabbed through her temple.

'It's only used occasionally these days. The gala will be the first time this year.'

'When is the gala?'

'About six weeks away.'

'And that's why I'm here.' She cocked her head in challenge. 'Isn't it?'

He cut across her. 'For the record, I like to keep a degree of separation between work and pleasure.'

While he spoke he had taken a step towards her, but in every other way he felt further away.

Humiliation swelled like a balloon inside her, but she didn't let it explode. 'That works for me.'

'I think you'll enjoy it.'

'Is this work we're talking about now?'

'I wouldn't have said it if we were not talking work, but unless you're a very good actress I know you enjoyed last night.'

She longed to throw his damned arrogance back in his beautiful smug face but he was right—she really wasn't that good an actress.

'The takeover we are celebrating was last month, but we felt it would be good to have a joint celebration for my grandfather's birthday also.'

'He'll be there too?' she blurted.

'Save your horror until after you have met him.'

'It's not horror, it's a genuine concern. I'm meant to be in charge of this thing, so a little more information would be useful.'

'I'll forward you the guest list. I think you'll know quite a few names on it, old friends and the like; it's a small world. I'm sure you'll enjoy catching up.'

But you're secretly hoping I won't, she thought, keeping her face blank. 'I won't be catching up with anyone; I'll be working.'

'Actually, the staff here will be supplemented by some outside caterers. Obviously, our kitchen—well, your kitchen,' he corrected with a slight smile, 'will be overseeing the menu. I would imagine it's not too late to make adjustments to your predecessor's arrangements if you want to put your own stamp on it, but your role will strictly be as executive chef, and as such you'll be expected to appear front of house.'

So that had been his plan all along: throw her in with a lot of people from her old life and introduce her as the hired help. 'How very not daunting at all,' she said drily.

His short, hard laugh echoed off the rafters. 'I think it would take a lot to daunt you.'

'Is that a compliment?'

Not an intentional one. On one level he knew that if he were objective he'd have been impressed by her resilience and her determination.

He wasn't objective.

'An observation,' he returned smoothly.

'Well, I won't be there. As I said, I'm very hands-on. I like to be in the kitchen at all times.'

'Hands-on…that's good to know,' he drawled smoothly and watched her blush like a virgin, which he knew she wasn't. He felt a stab of self-contempt. He had drawn the line in the sand, professional one side and personal the other, secure in the knowledge that all it took to blur that line was the scuff of a shoe.

'Besides, I don't have a thing to wear to that kind of occasion,' she rebutted, aware that her pounding head was not up to a full-scale battle on the subject—not now, anyway.

'I think we can fix that. I've always liked you in red.'

Amy clenched her teeth and resisted the temptation to rise to the bait. 'I don't want to be fixed or dressed.'

What about undressed? The thought formed in her head before she could stop it. In desperation, she changed the subject. 'Where does that hallway go?'

'There is access to the ramparts further along.' He gestured ahead. 'The view from the walk along them is worth seeing. But—' he glanced down at the sports watch on his wrist '——we'll need to cut the tour short as my grandfather is a creature of habit and routine, and since the pneumonia he usually rests before lunch.'

'I'm sorry, I didn't know he'd been ill.'

'He is not frail, but it takes a little longer to recover at his age.'

'I understand.'

'This way.'

She walked down the steps, wistfully imagining all the women in delicate heels and ballgowns who had gone before her. She frowned at herself and felt a surge of annoyance. She refused to feel envious of those Romano women, picked no doubt for their breeding and fortunes.

Once she had been a pale version of one of those women, expected to make a suitable alliance.

She felt sorry for them now.

She wasn't Leo's besotted lover.

She wasn't her parents' disappointment of a daughter.

She wasn't the rich girl who had been bought a restaurant.

She was just Amy, taking it one day at a time, and despite the worry over bills, the terror that her father would land himself back in prison, and the daily torment of being exposed to a man who made her remember she was actually a woman, she was happy to take responsibility for her own life.

Her hand slid down the smooth bannister. She had not belonged in the society that her parents had wanted her to inhabit, and this world that Leo navigated was so beyond that in every sense of the word. At least she had never been forced to be confronted by that reality at a time in her life when she would have struggled to cope.

If they had still been together when Leo had learnt of his Romano inheritance, an unlikely situation, given the limited shelf life of youthful passion, all it would have done was hasten the inevitable end.

Wealth changed people, and Leo would have left her behind.

But she was the one who had left him behind, and a man like Leo was always the one to walk away. What was going on between them now had a lot to do with bruised male ego. Nothing more. And that she could handle.

Her feet landed on the marble and she took a step back before Leo joined her.

'What is your grandfather like?'

Leo paused. 'He's like a man who threw his daughter away because, unlike you, she followed her heart.'

'Or her hormones?' she suggested, hiding layers of hurt under aggression, which came easy right now because the relief from generic painkillers had worn off and the telltale signs of an encroaching full-blown migraine were getting harder to ignore. 'And where did following her heart get her?'

'The situation is not comparable. My mother was pregnant and he drove her away. She was bringing up a child alone in a foreign country with no support.'

His empathy for his mother did him credit. Would he have been as empathetic if he had discovered she had unknowingly been carrying his child when they'd parted? It was a question she had asked herself many times over the years. Her instinct had made her want to run towards Leo, but maybe she was lucky she hadn't found him.

What if he had been horrified at being stuck with a

baby at his age? She felt the familiar ache as an image of a little boy with dark hair and Leo's eyes drifted into her head. Would he one day have children of his own?

'He gave her an ultimatum: dump the boyfriend or...'

'So they ran away together?' *Like we planned to do.* The thought made the empty space in her chest expand as, behind the tinted glasses she brought her lashes down in a silky shield so he wouldn't guess the comparison she was making, though he probably knew anyway.

But he'd never known about the baby. Never would, as what was the point in telling him now?

'No, he went back to his wife.'

She winced but closed her mouth over a sympathetic response. His expression suggested it would not have been well received.

'So your grandfather always knew he had a grand-child? When did he start looking for you?'

'No, he didn't know about me.' The admission sounded cold.

'So he didn't know your mother was pregnant?'

He flashed her a look. 'He sent her away because she wouldn't fall into line.'

In the same situation, she had stayed. She and Leo's mother were two sides of the same coin.

'I don't know your grandfather and I'm not defending him...' She shook her head and winced as the vice tightened around her chest. What could she say without revealing too much? 'Sorry, it's not my business. You obviously have a relationship, so that's good. It's not easy to let the past go, but you clearly understand one another.'

She almost added that you could always let the past

go, but then she realised that Leo was not a *let it go* sort of man.

He never forgave and never forgot.

CHAPTER EIGHT

'WHAT'S WRONG?'

'Nothing.'

'Then why are you hiding behind those sunglasses?'

'I'm not hiding, I have a headache.'

His brows lifted. 'Take an aspirin.'

'Empathy is one of your most endearing qualities,' she muttered, her sarcasm wasted on his broad back as she followed him along the echoing corridor, refusing to be distracted by the mad light show she was seeing the world through. Her brain foggy, she barely registered the network of rooms. She made a couple of grunting sounds when a response seemed to be indicated as she walked through open double doors.

Amy stayed where she was as Leo walked towards a figure sitting in a carved chair beside a window. Of course it was a window! Oh, God what was it with this place? Had no one told the architects that ancient castles were meant to be dark and gloomy?

Aware there was some uncharted swaying going on, Amy caught hold of the carved back of a chair to steady herself and waited, by this point not caring about what impression she made, like it mattered anyhow. She focused on what really mattered, which was not throwing up.

She caught snippets of the two men's conversation, not that it made much difference. They were speaking in Italian, which was perfectly natural and not part of some grand scheme to make her feel even more isolated, but the result was the same. On the bright side, if there was one, the room was not built on such cavernous proportions as many she had seen, though cosy would have been pushing it.

As she stared across at the figure sitting on the throne-like chair—not that he needed accessories to look regal—through a haze of shimmering lights, the delicate Italian greyhound dancing at his feet suddenly peeled away and trotted towards her.

'Good girl,' Amy whispered to the creature. She trailed her fingers for the dog to lick. 'I want to stroke you, I really do, but—' But if she bent down now the consequences might not be pretty, she finished in her head.

She was genuinely curious about the man that she had built in her head to be a fearful monster. She had anticipated he would be a big man but, unlike his grandson, he was smaller than average, almost slight, his dark hair heavily threaded with silver, his well-trimmed beard all silver. The only similarity she could detect was the hawklike nose.

His eyes appeared to be far lighter than Leo's and were set beneath grey-flecked, bushy brows. They swivelled her way and caught her staring.

He clicked his fingers and the dog at her feet ran, tail wagging, to his side...or was that click meant for her? Amy wondered.

'Chef!'

She flinched and half-closed her eyes. Whilst he was a relatively small man, his voice was not small at all, and the volume increased the pain in her skull. She tilted her head in cautious acknowledgement of the imperious summons and felt the room spin.

'The meal last night was quite acceptable. I go home tomorrow and, before I do, I wanted to thank you. My grandson is being quite mysterious about where he found you.' He flashed a look at Leo, who simply raised an eyebrow in response.

Watching them face off, Amy struggled to work out what they reminded her of—before it came to her.

'Like two silverbacks,' she murmured, not really aware she had voiced her observation out loud until both men turned their heads to stare at her.

Whether they minded being compared to two gorillas minus the chest-beating was not a priority, because Amy's priority was finding a bathroom.

'Actually, could you point me in the direction of—' Her hand clamped to her mouth, she looked around desperately.

Leo appeared to take in the situation at a glance. 'This way.'

Hovering outside the bathroom door, Leo's face twisted into a grimace of sympathy and concern as he listened to the sounds coming from inside. He had never seen anyone look as pale as Amy had looked as he had half-carried her to the nearest bathroom.

The sounds seemed to have subsided and when he cautiously opened the door this time all he heard was running water. No voice yelling, *'Go away!'* like the two previous times he had attempted to invade the space. Not that it would have mattered; he had already decided that enough was enough and he wasn't going away.

He stepped inside the room, alarm shooting through him as he saw the small figure sitting cross-legged on the floor. He switched off the tap that was still gushing water before he squatted down beside her. She was grey now rather than white. He felt a pang inside his chest that hurt, even though he had long ago conquered the tender protectiveness she evoked in him.

She had done him a favour, actually. He could now enjoy sex with no emotional connection. Because it was not the sex that was dangerous, it was the emotions. That had been a life-changing discovery and he had Amy to thank for it.

'Are you all right?'

Morning sickness. Out of nowhere, the thought took root in his head.

She couldn't be pregnant.

Why shouldn't she be?

The idea that Amy was carrying another man's baby was not one he could contemplate. It was a rejection that had nothing to do with logic and everything to do with the irrational emotions he had banished from his life.

The same way Amy had banished him. Now she was back—and he had brought her back. He had slept with her and the more contact they had, the less his reasons for bringing her here made sense. He was meant to be congratulating himself on having escaped a weak, spine-less creature, sure she would reveal her true self when the props were removed.

Well, that's working out well for you, isn't it? Leo mocked himself.

What Amy lacked in inches she more than made up for in guts and sheer determination, not to mention sheer bloody-mindedness.

When she gave no indication that she had heard him, he repeated his question. 'Are you all right?'

Amy batted away his hand. For an intelligent man, he asked some very stupid questions. 'No.'

'Can you open your eyes?'

'I could but I don't want to,' she mumbled through clenched teeth. 'Will you just leave me alone with my splitting head and let me die in peace?'

He snorted. 'You're not going to die.'

She considered the response inhuman.

'This is a headache?' He couldn't keep the doubt out of his voice.

'No, it's not a bloody headache, it's a migraine. It's a headache like a tornado is a gentle breeze.'

Listening to her response, at how Amy managed to pack an incredible amount of aggression and loathing into a whisper, Leo felt something painful break loose in his chest. She was so fragile and yet so tough.

'I'll take you to your room. Can you walk? Oh, I know you can, but you don't have to.'

'My balance goes.'

'Not a problem.' He bent down to scoop her up.

'You can't carry me,' she whimpered as her head, which she couldn't hold up, found the support of his shoulder, and she discovered another scent that did not make her feel queasy—Leo.

'Actually, I can.'

And he did, although the journey was all a bit of a blur to Amy as they negotiated a myriad of corridors and passageways.

Lying on her bed in a blissfully dark room, she made objections when someone who she didn't want to identify but knew was Leo unlaced her trainers.

She grunted and rolled into a foetal ball of misery.

'The doctor will be here presently.'

'I don't need a doctor. I just need you to go away.'

'You are a very bad patient.'

The unexpected tenderness in his voice made her eyes seep weak tears that ran silently and unchecked down her cheeks before blotting into the pillow.

'Ah, here he is now. I will leave you.'

She wanted to yell *Don't go*...but, ashamed of her weakness, she managed to stop herself. She was not so incapacitated that she had lost sight of the fact that safety was the last thing that Leo represented. Not to her, anyway.

The doctor was gentle and kind, he didn't drag out the consultation and the only questions he asked were pertinent.

He told her he would arrange a prescription for her normal medication should this happen again.

The jab he gave her, he explained, would deal with her nausea, vomiting and pain.

'You just need some quiet and to sleep.'

She didn't really expect to sleep, but when the door closed and she was alone, able to lower her defences virtually immediately, she did fall into a deep sleep.

When she woke, her initial disorientation morphed

into relief as she registered that the hammer inside her skull was now just faint background noise.

At the first little groan she emitted, Leo rose from his seat by the window and laid down his laptop. By the time he reached the bed, Amy was levering herself awkwardly into a sitting position.

'Don't—let me,' he said, masking his concern under a layer of brusque irritation. He recognised that his irritation was ridiculous, given that the entire object of this exercise had been—what? Revenge? To make her feel vulnerable and uncomfortable? But he'd never been aiming for torture, which was what her pain level had apparently been.

Of course, she could have simply admitted the problem, explain that she was unwell, but it seemed to him that this Amy admitted nothing, certainly not to him anyway. She had looked so damned vulnerable and fragile as she'd slept, her dark lashes spread like butterflies' wings on her scarily pale cheeks.

He had countered any feelings of irrational guilt on his part by focusing on the blindingly obvious. Which was that Amy was the author of this situation, simply by not owning up to a weakness and also not bringing essential medication with her.

Did it not occur to her that he had better things to do than keep a bedside vigil?

Nobody asked you to, the annoying voice in his head argued. *You could have delegated.*

'Like I have a choice,' Amy muttered, leaning against the conveniently placed pillow behind her back. Then gritted out a grudging, 'Thank you, but I'm not an invalid.'

He tilted his dark head in mocking acknowledgment. 'You're most welcome.' He scanned her face, the sarcastic glint in his heavy-lidded eyes fading as he took in her pallor and the violet smudges beneath her eyes, hating that he had no control over the surge of protectiveness, an emotional response he thought he'd left behind nine years ago.

This was the woman who had ripped out his heart and stomped all over it. What the hell was he doing or, more importantly, feeling?

'So, how are you feeling?' The ice clinked in the jug as he poured her a glass of water and passed it to her.

She looked at it without reacting.

'Employment law frowns on employees not being hydrated.'

She huffed out a sigh and took the glass because her mouth and throat were dry.

He watched as, holding it in two hands, she glugged the liquid greedily.

'Slowly, you don't want to throw up again.'

The reminder made her pull the glass from her lips and set it down on the bedside table. 'I'm not going to—' In the act of flinging off the throw that had been laid across her legs, her eyes widened with horror as a pained version of the morning's events flashed through her head. *Oh, God, talk about first impressions!*

'Your grandfather—'

'He is grateful you didn't throw up on his shoes.'

'I'm glad you think this is a joke. He didn't really say that, did he?'

'No. The two of you should get on; his sense of humour is a little underdeveloped too. Don't worry, he took it in his stride and has decided to blame me for the entire incident. And as I couldn't make myself available to dance attendance on him, he has left early. He never stays long, though. It was hard for him to relinquish the reins in the first instance.'

'Was he really all right about it?'

Leo sighed. 'Actually, he suggested I sack you.'

This professional insult roused her from her lethargy. 'I'm a better chef than you deserve!'

'He's decided you're pregnant.'

She was unprepared for that and had no defence against the bleakness that washed over her in a wave.

'I'm not. And as it's unlikely I'll ever see your grandfather again, I'd be grateful if you'd tell him that. Also, employment law means you couldn't sack me even if I was.'

'You will see him at the gala.'

'I'm not going to allow you to wheel me out like a prize example of how the mighty have fallen.'

He bit back a retort, aware that he had an unfair advantage here. He wasn't as weak as a kitten—a kitten with claws, he thought, making that all-important clarification.

'He's a bit of a foodie and he loves talking about food. He says, at his age, food is better than sex. Apparently, this is something I have to look forward to, but for the moment food is simply fuel.'

'What about sex?' The words tripped off her tongue before she could stop them.

'Sex is one of the joys of life.' He could imagine a man finding sex with Amy to be one of life's necessities, like oxygen. A man who was not him, of course, as he was a man who was never going to care enough to be hurt again.

Only Leo could turn a conversation about food into one about sex and make it sound so impersonal.

'You're obsessed,' she accused.

'Maybe we both are, and you introduced the subject.' Head tilted to one side, he stood back and surveyed her burning face. 'Now you're looking a much better colour; you have some warmth in your cheeks.'

She flung him a killer glare. 'Why,' she added, swinging her legs over the side of the bed, 'are you even in here?'

He was watching her progress with a critical frown. 'I'm delivering the medication, as per your doctor's instructions.' He nodded to the parcel on her bedside table. 'He tells me that, taken early enough, these usually stop the progress of a migraine.'

'Mostly.'

'You, I understand, did not bring your own medication.'

She slung him an irritated look, not appreciating the preachy tone he had adopted, as if she were some recalcitrant six-year-old. She toyed with the idea of just flicking him the finger and crawling back under the covers. It was a non-starter as options went but thinking about it tugged the corners of her mouth upwards into an almost smile.

'I had to leave the house in rather a rush.' She bit down on her lower lip. Damn him, she even *sounded* like a six-year-old now!

Their child would have been eight now.

It was several years too late for a big reveal, which

she was glad of, as the idea of telling Leo filled her with icy horror.

She had tried once, though… When she had discovered she was pregnant, the first thing she had done was to ring him. But her call, and the many that had followed, had been blocked.

So she had packed a bag and decided to follow him. Tell him he was going to be a father.

It was a measure of her panic and desperation that she had ever imagined that was a sane idea. Not after the way he had left. She hadn't really thought the plan through; actually, she hadn't had a plan at all. She had been running to him on pure instinct, more homing pigeon than sane person.

Except, of course, Leo had never been her home, although having him here, looking out for her, she couldn't help but imagine what her life would have been like if he had.

Life hadn't disillusioned her enough to make her lose the belief that a person could be your home—the right person. She just no longer believed she would find the right person for her.

As time had gone on, it had grown increasingly unlikely. Besides, her work had never allowed for a lot of dating and the men who asked her out usually wanted to use her to advance their careers, when she had been in a position to do so.

But she had tried to do the right thing, despite how hard it was. She'd left a note for her parents, telling them not to worry and she'd be in touch. She had been on a train going to London when the cramps had kicked in.

She had made it back home again before her parents

had found the note. Other than the hospital staff and the cleaner who had found the discarded hospital identity bracelet in her bedroom and silently handed it to her, and hugged her, she had told nobody.

'Are you all right?'

Amy pulled her head up cautiously but still managed to loosen another hank of silky pillow-tousled hair. 'Fine,' she said giving up with a sigh of frustration on refastening her braid. Instead, she began to remove some of the remaining hairpins, lining them up on the bedside table before sliding her fingers into the already unravelling braid to loosen it.

'If you want me to admit it's my fault that I almost threw up on your grandfather's shoes, then fine—mea culpa,' she said, continuing to work on her hair, which had been damp when she had fastened it and now fell in a mass of Pre-Raphaelite ripples down her back.

Sensing he was watching her, she looked up, and there was something compulsive in his stare that sent her stomach muscles into a nosedive.

'Why don't you wear it loose any more?'

'I work in a kitchen, so it's a matter of health and safety. I actually cut it a few years ago, but it was more work keeping it—' She stopped, thinking, *Oh, yes, Amy, because your hair down the years is a really fascinating subject.*

'You have beautiful hair.' The stark delivery, combined with the mesmerising heat in his stare, added another layer to the rapidly thickening atmosphere.

'I remember you sitting astride me and your hair brushing my chest—' He halted, his smoky stare managing to be fierce but also soft and seductive.

Amy stopped breathing. She was shaking, except she wasn't. The tremor was not superficial; it was deep inside her.

Remember?

She remembered crying herself to sleep for days and weeks and months. And she remembered feeling utterly bereft, never sharing her secret, her grief, with anyone, because there was no one to share it with.

She had wanted Leo so much. Him being here now, looking out for her, brought home just how badly she had needed him back then too.

'I try not to relive the past, Leo.' Because it hurt too damned much. 'That's why none of *this* is a very good idea.'

'I'm not trying to relive the past. I'm trying to exorcise it and the ghosts and enjoy the present.'

She stared, fascinated by the magnificent symmetry of his face as it tightened, pulling the gold-toned skin across his perfect bones, before his expression changed and he produced a charisma-loaded smile, his eyes gleaming through his ludicrously long eyelashes.

'In fact, I think we should enjoy it together.'

CHAPTER NINE

AMY STARED STRAIGHT AHEAD. She barely came up to his shoulder, so his chest was straight ahead. A trick of the light, the fineness of the shirt fabric or her wilful imagination, but she could see the suggestion of a sprinkling of dark hair. It sparked tactile images of her fingers stroking the hair-roughened satiny skin, tracing the ridges of muscle on his flat belly, before…

This was crazy! She was not a particularly sexual person—and certainly not someone who allowed dark fantasies to take over. It had only ever happened with Leo. It didn't take any effort on his part; all he had to do was breathe to bypass all her defences.

It had always been Leo.

'In bed, you mean. You're not interested in me anywhere else.'

'I was thinking more of a walk in the fresh air, but…'

She flushed. 'I should be in work.'

'No one is expecting you today.'

His hand slid down her back, the featherlight contact sending electric flutters of sensation along her spine before his fingers came to rest lightly on her waist.

She told herself he'd pushed in closer but it was a lie; she had done the pushing and all the denial in the world wasn't going to change the fact. He held up his arm to reveal the slim, silver-banded watch he wore on his wrist, displaying a light sprinkling of fine dark hair as he flicked the cuff to display a sinewy forearm.

'It's five thirty-four.'

He dropped his arm, shifted his stance and the brain-debilitating contact was broken. It took a few deep breaths for her to fight clear of the sexual thrall that had immobilised her.

Amy cleared her throat and met his eyes, her defiance slipping several notches when she read the total understanding gleaming there. She knew that he knew *exactly* what he was doing to her, and she wanted to crawl away and hide.

'You shred my control too, you know that.'

He voiced the devastating truth almost casually, but there was nothing casual about the muscle clenching and unclenching in his lean cheek, visible through the shadow of stubble that hadn't been there earlier.

Amy breathed through the heart-thudding, shocking moment and, before she had formulated any sort of response, he moved towards the door in a dizzying change of direction in his body language and his voice.

'Even I don't jump on women who have just got out of their sick bed.' Which didn't mean he wasn't tempted. 'How about I let you freshen up and have something light to eat sent up? Then we will explore the grounds. It might put some colour in your cheeks.'

Amy knew she had plenty of colour; her cheeks were still burning in fiery reaction.

'There's no need for you to do all that.'

'But I don't trust you—' He paused, his glance landing for a few tense moments on her mouth.

'Trust me to do what?'

'To not return to the kitchen and get in everyone's way. They're already aware of the situation.'

'You mean they know you're blackmailing me?'

'No, that we're having sex.'

She went white then saw the unholy amusement in his eyes and cursed. 'Was that meant to be a joke?'

'Would it be so bad if they did know?'

She regarded him incredulously. 'Too right it would! And it was sex in the singular!'

'The day is still young, but I actually meant that they know you're unwell.'

'Being unwell cuts no ice in a kitchen, believe you me.'

'Yes, I'm sure you are very tough, and well able to drag yourself to work with a broken leg or share your flu with your colleagues. But being unwell *does* cut ice in this kitchen when I make it clear to everyone that you are to rest and recuperate.'

'That sounds like an abuse of power.'

He breathed out a sigh and folded his arms across his chest as he looked down at her. 'That's an interesting take on an employer who looks after the welfare of his workforce.'

Amy decided that this was the point when it made sense to stop digging the hole she was sinking into while she could still climb out. She bit her lip and pointed out, 'I have rested.'

She still couldn't get over the fact that she had slept so much of the day away.

'I think it will take more than a couple of hours to re-dress the fact that you appear to have been functioning on the edge of exhaustion for weeks, possibly months…'

'So you brought me here for a holiday?'

He reacted to her sarcasm with a frown as he raked a hand through his dark hair. 'At this point I don't know why the hell I brought you here!'

She was still blinking when the door closed behind him with a forceful click.

CHAPTER TEN

WHEN AMY CAME out of the bathroom in a fresh change of clothes she could see through the opening into the sitting room that the tea tray and sandwiches that had been delivered earlier by a fresh-faced maid had been removed.

She felt a lot better, though she was reluctant to acknowledge her relief that she wasn't due in the kitchen.

She sat down in front of the mirror and opened her make-up bag, but after a reflective moment closed it, having extracted some lip gloss. She didn't want to make it look like she was trying too hard—or, for that matter, trying at all.

She never wanted to be like her mother, desperate to please a man. Getting up at the crack of dawn so her husband wasn't offended by her face without make-up, and splashing cash on the latest craze to eliminate any signs of ageing.

It didn't take her long to braid her hair into one thick plait, which she threw over her shoulder. About to get up, she paused and unzipped the make-up bag again, deciding that a smudge of neutral eyeshadow and a flick of a mascara wand couldn't really be considered *trying hard*.

At the tap on the door she took a moment to compose

herself, which wasn't so easy when her heart was drumming so hard she could feel it in her throat.

Amy had reached the door, where a steadying breath and being ninety-nine percent sure of who would be on the other side didn't prevent her experiencing the shockwave impact of seeing Leo standing there.

Brain numb, her senses so acute it hurt, she stayed glued to the spot.

'You look…' His eyes flickered down her slim figure, taking in the narrowness of her waist in the full-skirted cotton. The butter-yellow of the sleeveless bodice made the golden-brown of her eyes pop. 'Better.'

'Better than bedraggled is not a high bar, but I'll take it,' she said pertly, flinging back the braid that landed in the middle of her back.

'I like the fifties vibe of your dress.'

'Thanks,' she said lightly, closing the door behind her as she stepped out into the wide corridor. 'How?' she wondered, looking at the view through the window. 'You have the sea view this side and through the bedroom window.' She turned to glance at the door to her suite, which faced in the opposite direction. 'Did I somehow miss the bridge? We're not on an island, are we?'

'No, a peninsula, so we look out on the Tyrrhenian Sea from all sides.'

'It's an incredible place.'

'A long way from my bedsit above the garage with the view of the petrol pumps.'

Amy turned away; she didn't want to think about the stolen moments they had shared in that poky bedsit. Peeling wallpaper and threadbare carpet notwithstanding, they were the only times in her life when she had experienced true happiness. 'I could do with some fresh air.'

Leo didn't comment on the hint of desperation in her overly bright response. 'This way.'

He led her in the direction Amy recalled as being the route from the kitchens, but before they reached the stone staircase he led her into a lift.

'If you want to go out, this is your quickest route.' Unlike her, he appeared oblivious to the skin-peeling tension in the enclosed space. Tension that made her virtually throw herself out when the doors swished open.

Directly opposite, a solid metal-banded oak door was open and she stepped out into the early evening sunshine and paused to take in her surroundings.

She was standing in a courtyard. The space was filled with the trickle of water and the hum of bees that hovered above the lavender which spilled from the raised beds and the wild thyme that grew in the cracks in the stone-gravelled footpaths. There were a couple of wrought iron benches and tables set beside a fountain. The stone walls of the castle were on three sides, leaving the south-facing fourth side open to a vista that was breathtaking. It must make this a sun trap most of the day, she thought.

The area directly ahead sloped, the green manicured lawn giving way to immaculate terrace gardens where flowers spilled from several beds onto what appeared to be a grove of olives. Through the foliage she caught glimpses of what she took to be a white sandy beach beyond. The blue of the sea itself was almost indistinguishable from the blue sky.

'This is so beautiful.' She didn't bother disguising her uncomplicated admiration for the beauty of the place.

Despite herself, she felt excited at the prospect of exploration.

'This way.'

Her feet crunched on the gravel as he led her out of the courtyard and onto the grassy expanse of the lawn. She turned around and looked back at the castle, her full skirt skimming her calves as she twirled.

Despite the reason for her being here, and the man whose presence by her side meant that she couldn't totally relax, she laughed, unable to regret experiencing this place.

She just regretted the reason she was here.

He wasn't sure what he'd expected her reaction to be, but her laughter and her almost childlike pleasure in her surroundings was not it.

He fought off a smile—her uncomplicated delight was contagious. 'You like it?'

She flashed him a look, her face a mirror of her amused astonishment. 'That's a joke, right? It's beautiful, Leo, and I'm happy for you that you have such a beautiful home.'

His own expression blanked as he searched her face, but he saw nothing but genuine sincerity.

Underneath his composed expression, his jaw was practically hitting his chest. What sort of woman got treated the way he had treated her and then pronounced herself *happy* for him?

'It must be like living in a fairytale.'

'I do not believe in fairytales or happily ever after endings.'

And that was how to kill the moment! Was she in part responsible for his inbuilt cynicism? The possibility drained away the last of her optimism and left her feeling flat as she walked on.

Seeing the happiness fade from her face sent a slug of irrational guilt through Leo. 'This way,' he said when she had wandered off aimlessly towards the right.

Amy was standing above the highest level of the numerous terraces when Leo, standing below her, turned and held out his hand. She regarded it suspiciously for a moment before laying her own lightly on his. Leo turned his hand and interlaced his fingers within hers and took the first step.

'It's a bit of a drop for—'

'The vertically challenged?'

'I wasn't going to say that.'

'You were thinking it,' she snapped back, recalling his racing stable of tall leggy blondes. 'Though,' she added with a conciliatory smile, 'I'm glad I didn't wear heels. This,' she went on as she followed the narrow path that connected the layers of lush greenery and brilliant blooms, 'is mountain goat country.'

'Do you want to sit down for a while?' he asked as they reached a gazebo. A couple of stone cherubs on the wall behind them gushed bubbling water into the trough below the stone seat, and behind it irises grew in profusion in the mossy ground. It was a cool and calm spot.

'No, I'm fine, thanks.' She caught sight of the name engraved in the stone seat. '*Luisa Romano,*' she read. 'Your mother?'

He nodded though his body language had already indicated her guess had been correct.

'It's very beautiful.'

'Simple. I'm no designer, but I like to work with my

hands.' He held up his hands, his long fingers splayed for a moment.

Amy remembered how skilled those hands were and felt her insides dissolve. So she rushed into speech. 'I didn't know you could do self-deprecating.'

His laugh lowered the tension by several degrees.

'This,' he said, running his fingers across the stone surface, 'was one of our bonding moments.'

Her brow puckered at the cynicism in his voice. 'You and your grandfather?' she asked cautiously.

'We try, but the history makes it hard.'

The flicker of pained anguish in his eyes was there and gone, maybe even imagined on her part, but Amy's tender heart clenched in her chest.

He turned his head and saw the empathy shining in her eyes. This woman wore her feelings so close to the surface she might as well wear a sign saying, *I'm a soft touch—take advantage of me.*

Which, of course, he was.

His jaw tightened as he experienced a fresh stab of guilt.

'Maybe I could actually do with a rest,' she murmured, sliding onto the bench. It was a simple repurposed slab of stone, worn smooth with age. While the area was now out of the sun, it retained the warmth of earlier in the day and she could feel the heat through the cotton of her skirt.

After a moment Leo joined her. He sat beside her but apart.

'Sounds like you've both put some effort in,' she observed softly.

'There isn't an ocean between us, but I still wouldn't

like to swim it.' He stopped dead. She was wandering around in his head and the hell of it was that he had invited her into it—actually, he was giving her the guided tour.

What on earth was he doing?

'Are you a good swimmer?' She swivelled sideways to look at him, thinking he was definitely more handsome than any man had the right to be. He was certainly built for swimming and she could easily imagine him, streamlined and sleek, cutting through the water.

Leo turned his head and captured her gaze. 'Better since I moved here. The sea, the pool, are perfect opportunities to improve technique and stamina. My technique has, I like to think, improved greatly over the years.'

She intercepted the challenging carnal gleam in his eyes and the message wasn't exactly subtle. Subtle or not, she was helpless to resist, a sexual flush travelling over her skin until the rosy tide had suffused every tingling inch of her body.

Amy shook her head, willing her panicked heartbeat to slow as she pushed her hands into the deep pockets of her skirt to disguise the fact they were trembling.

'That is a very obvious deflection,' she managed coolly as she got to her feet and brushed down her skirt.

He arched a brow. 'From where I'm standing—'

And he was standing now, the difference in their heights immediately putting her at a disadvantage.

'It looks like it was a pretty good deflection. You going to blame that on the temperature?' he wondered, looking directly at her breasts under the yellow top.

She didn't need to look to know her treacherous body

was betraying her, but at least not all of her giveaways were as prominent as her tight nipples.

'Has it occurred to you, Amy, that you're not exactly the best person to be handing out family advice?'

She flinched as his hit landed, her eyes widening in protest at the suggestion. 'I am not handing out advice. I was trying to figure out why you are such a bastard.'

'Oh, I'm a self-made man,' he drawled through bared teeth. 'Of course, I have had a little bit of help along the way.'

Her lips clamped tight. He never lost an opportunity to turn the knife, did he? But part of her didn't blame him.

She shrugged, her eyes straying once more to the en-graved name on the bench before she stepped out of the shaded area and into the warm evening sun. 'You'd probably be happier if you let go of the past.' She tossed the words over her shoulder and walked ahead of him, making her way down the rows of terraces, all the time aware of his footsteps behind her, though he made no attempt to join her.

He had spoilt her pleasure in the beauty of her sur-roundings.

She had reached the flat ground that led onto the copse of olives when he caught up with her.

'That path leads to the beach, or do you want to go back?'

Amy was torn. She could have said something sting-ing, along the lines of her voluntarily spending more time in his company was about as likely as…well, something that was very unlikely.

On the other hand, she had really wanted to see the

sea up close ever since her first glimpse of it. Now she could smell it and the draw was impossible to resist.

She wasn't aware she had sighed until she glanced up and saw the sardonic amusement painted on his dark fallen-angel features as he watched her struggle.

It was very hard to shake the conviction that he could read her like a book. It wasn't a two-way situation; he remained frustratingly enigmatic.

Trawling through her recollections, Amy realised he always had been, really. He had given out very little information in the past, and she hadn't pushed him for anything back then because the mysteriousness of him had fed her romantic fantasies.

'I'll be masterful and take charge, shall I? Beach.' He gestured to the path off to the left.

After a short pause she followed, walking behind him between the straight lines of the trees. It was cool and quiet except for her frantic heartbeat as she surveyed the movements of the tall figure up ahead.

She had been determined to maintain a cool silence but, as they walked on, the idea felt childish. Also, the need to fill the silence grew impossible to resist.

'Do you produce your own olive oil?'

'We do, but this area is no longer commercial. We have productive groves to the south on the mountain slopes. This part is actually a little neglected, hence why the wild perennial flowers underfoot have taken hold.'

'They are pretty.'

'It's tough to control them without using herbicides, which bring their own issues; it's ultimately about sustainability and, of course, the health of the land.'

A frown appeared between her brows as she flung her

plait back, waving her hand to deter the insects buzzing around her face. 'I didn't realise that you took such
a personal interest in the estate. I thought you were just
about—'

He paused and turned back, looking at her with his
usual mocking grin. 'Making money?' His smile faded.
'Did you use some insect repellant?'

'I didn't think I'd need it.'

'Well, you will.'

'I think they like me,' she admitted, swatting her arm.

'Come on.'

The pace he set for the next few yards felt more like
a jog for Amy but when they emerged onto the beach all
thought of complaining faded.

The wide curved stretch of white, sugary sand was
empty, and the sun reflecting off the turquoise-streaked
sea was dazzling.

He watched as her wide smile emerged, her pleasure
and excitement unfeigned.

'This is simply incredible.'

'Take off your shoes; the sand gets everywhere.'

She saw that Leo had already kicked off his shoes. He
stood there in his cut-offs and a tee-shirt that exposed
his impressive biceps, looking very much at home and a
million miles away from the images of him which were
distributed for PR purposes. And even further from the
man usually seen on red carpets with his arm around
beautiful blondes.

The sea looked so tempting that she sighed as she
walked across the hot sand to the water's edge. 'I should
have brought my swimsuit,' she mourned.

'You don't need a swimsuit; there's nobody here.'

She could not allow the provocation to pass or, for that matter, for the pleasure of the moment to be ruined.

'You're here.'

'I can fade into the background.' He touched the tee-shirt stretched over his broad chest. 'See, camouflage.'

She threw back her head and laughed. The idea of Leo fading into any background, anywhere, in any circumstances was one of the funniest things she had ever heard.

He watched as she wiped tears from her cheeks, her laughter morphing before his eyes into broken sobs that lifted her chest.

'Amy...?'

Her eyes went from his outstretched hand to his face, which was creased with a wary, quizzical expression that indicated she must look like lunatic. She pressed a hand to her mouth in an attempt to physically suppress any further outbursts and took some gulping breaths, mortified by the unrestrained spillage of suppressed emotions.

'It could be worse; I could be crying.'

He felt a surge of empathy shake free inside him and sidestepped it, not ready to accept his own feelings—the feelings she shook loose in him.

'Are you waiting for me to do empathy?'

She swallowed a bubble of laughter. 'Don't, or you'll set me off again. It's the migraine; it can leave me feeling a bit...'

Insane.

In lust.

In deep, deep trouble.

'Let's get you back to the house.'

'Castle,' she was unable to stop herself correcting. 'And I can get myself back.'

'Give me strength.' He would certainly need it, he decided as he watched her tramp with a gentle sway of her hips up the sand, the full skirt of her yellow dress whipping around her legs in the sea breeze.

He had brought her here thinking of revenge, never dreaming that what he was really doing was locking himself in a room with a live, primed sexual grenade.

Another school of thought, jeered the voice in his head, *is that you knew exactly what you were doing, Leo.*

She'd hurt him once; only a fool would invite her to take a second shot. And he wasn't a fool.

'I wasn't offering to carry you, *cara*.' And he wasn't offering her another shot at his heart either. 'Once in one day is enough; you are more solid than you look.'

Determined not to give him the satisfaction of responding, she twisted her lips and stalked off.

There was no cosy conversation during the return walk; there wasn't even any confrontational conversation. The couple of glances she risked throwing in Leo's direction suggested that his thoughts were elsewhere.

'Will you be able to find your way back to your suite?' he asked when they reached the big oak door.

'Of course,' she replied with a calm confidence she was far from feeling. 'Thank you for the guided tour.'

'We hardly scraped the surface, but I'll arrange for someone to give you the full tour soon.'

Someone, not him. She got the message and obviously she was glad.

'We thought you'd prefer to have your dinner in your room.'

She assumed the *we* was him, but she said nothing. She didn't even point out that someone could have enquired about her preference, which required great restraint on her part.

He made to move away and stopped. 'Oh, the garden lighting on the beach paths is temporarily out of service for some repairs. So if you do decide during the week to take any night air, stick to the gardens around the castle. The kitchen garden is that way and the tennis courts and swimming pools are just a little further on.'

She tipped her head in acknowledgement and walked in through the double doors without looking back.

She was waiting when her dinner was served.

The maid looked startled to be greeted by Amy, who took the tray and joined her in the hallway. 'I think I'd prefer to eat with company in the kitchen.'

Her appearance was greeted with surprise and more sympathy than Amy had anticipated, as she assured them that she wasn't here to work.

'I was going a bit mad just talking to myself.'

There were fewer staff than the previous day, which made sense. Apparently, they were only serving two—plus the staff—who, from what she saw, ate very well.

As she sat on a stool eating the really delicious monkfish kebabs with a crunchy side salad and subtle tikka sauce, watching the interplay between the staff, several of them came across to talk for a moment or two.

Conversation was about food, with a bit of juicy gossip thrown in for good measure, and Amy found herself relaxing for the first time since she'd arrived.

Occasionally, she glanced towards the door, wondering what Leo's reaction would be if he discovered she had ignored his edict to stay in her room. Well, maybe not an *edict,* but he had been extremely high-handed. If he had appeared, she would have told him so, not that she was looking for a fight—or him.

She would have liked to linger in the kitchen, but it felt wrong to be there and not work and she was feeling extremely tired again, which was often the way if she allowed a migraine to develop.

When she went to carry her tray over to the dishwashers it was firmly taken off her.

Amy didn't protest; she was actually quite touched by the kindness.

Would she have been so touched if Leo had been the one offering the kindness? The inconvenient question stayed in her head as she made her way back to her own suite.

It wasn't *what* he said; it was the *way* he said it.

The next time she saw him she would tell him so, she decided tiredly before she lay down in bed. She was asleep before her head hit the pillow.

She didn't actually see Leo all the next day; he did not put in a disruptive appearance in the kitchen or highjack her along the long hallways. There was no request for her presence, which meant her day was harassment-free and rather productive.

The evening meal left the pass looking like a work of art and she knew it tasted as good as it looked. There was, after all, no harm being a perfectionist.

She ate supper with the rest of the staff and they discussed their own individual versions of French meringue, as retro floating islands were making a comeback on menus.

The idea of the sea drew her, and the draw had nothing whatever to do with a childish impulse to ignore Leo's instructions. The summer days were long and she would be back at the castle before darkness fell.

She thought she might have met someone as she trod the same path she had yesterday, but it was both deserted and silent, except for when the noise of a helicopter above made her look up and watch until it vanished behind the forested area to the east, presumably to land in the same place she had when they'd arrived.

Would there be more guests to feed tomorrow? Courtesy of the kitchen gossip, she had learnt that Leo's female companions never visited the castle. He appeared to keep his life strictly compartmentalised.

Amy took a few moments when she reached the beach to drink in the view. Leo had said he swam here but, not being the strongest swimmer in the world, she had taken the precaution of checking the tides and asking about any dangerous currents.

It took her a few moments to pull off the wraparound skirt and her white cotton top and arrange them neatly on top of the canvas bag containing her towel and the book she had brought.

The sand was warm underfoot as she ran down to the sea.

She was happy to paddle for a little while, meandering up and down the beach in the warm, crystal-clear water before she walked out until she was deep enough to swim. Her slow breaststroke was never going to break any records and she was careful to keep parallel to the beach and not go out of her depth, until she grew tired and flipped over onto her back to float lazily, seeing the sun through the delicate skin of her eyelids. With just the hiss of the waves breaking on the shore and the odd bird screeching overhead, she felt her cares and tensions slip away.

She eventually opened her eyes and wondered if too much relaxing was bad for you. She had floated further out than she'd intended and was, without a doubt, out of her depth. But it wasn't *too* far.

She didn't allow herself to panic, though it was nipping at her heels as she determinedly set off for the shore. It seemed to take an incredibly long time to reach the shallows and stand on her feet, water streaming down her body, her heart hammering with a combination of the physical effort and relief as she waded to the shore.

She spread out her towel and collapsed onto it, lying there with her ribcage lifting in tune with her rapid exhalations, which gradually slowed as the relaxing heat seeped into her limbs. Her adrenaline levels lowered as she closed her eyes.

It wasn't cold, but it was the perceptible change in temperature that woke her. She sat up and looked around, initially confused before she realised that she had fallen asleep. There was no sun; instead, the beach was lit by moonlight and the sea was now silver-streaked and dark, and was lapping only a few feet away from her.

She ransacked her bag to find her phone and gasped when she saw the time. It was close on midnight. Scrambling to her feet and swearing under her breath, she struggled into her top and then fastened her skirt over her bikini, which was now bone-dry. Even her rope of hair, which usually took an age to dry, was barely damp.

Retaining her phone before pushing everything else

into her bag, she slung it over her shoulder and headed for the trees. Without the moonlight and the light of her phone it would have been pitch-black. Even with these light sources, the olive grove felt very different than in daylight, the trees' skeletal outlines in the dark seeming sinister and unwelcoming. Heart pounding, she began to run, every snap of a twig and animal call raising her heart rate.

It was a relief to emerge, but she didn't pause. Jogging across the flat ground, she didn't stop until she reached the lowest terrace.

Her nervousness now seemed foolish with the soothing aroma of night-scented stocks and roses filling the air. She wasn't in a wilderness; she was a few hundred metres from a building with dozens of people in it. Though it might have been better to have remembered that she wasn't afraid of the dark five minutes ago.

By the time she reached the third level, the illuminated castle came into view and the last of the tension bunching her shoulders loosened. She even took the time out to linger a little to admire the spotlit iconic building.

CHAPTER ELEVEN

'I CAN'T DECIDE if you're stupid or stubborn!'

Amy screamed and spun around, fists raised, to face the owner of the voice, who seemed to materialise out of the undergrowth, a dark, sinister shadow looming over her.

Then the darkness was broken by a powerful beam of light that made her blink, and the dark figure took form and shape.

Feeling stupid, she hit out with a querulous, 'What are you doing? You gave me the fright of my life!'

'What am *I* doing?' he barked.

'Get that thing out of my eyes!'

Not just out of her eyes but out of the way full stop, and the darkness descended again. Other senses compensated when you couldn't see. And her well-developed sense of smell was busy compensating. Amy tried and failed not to breathe in the clean male scent Leo exuded.

The dark was dangerous, but the danger that lurked in the shadows wasn't ghouls or ghosts. People did things in the dark that they wouldn't do in daylight; it freed up inhibitions, not that she'd ever had any of those where Leo was concerned.

'Can we skip the part where you work yourself up

into a foot-stamping temper tantrum, because it isn't going to alter the fact you are in the wrong. I explained that this area was off-limits at night until the electricity supply is—'

She made a scornful noise in her throat. 'There is no light issue; the place is lit up like a Christmas tree.' She was making a pointy-fingered gesture to the brightly lit castle when the lights went out, along with the moon.

'You were saying?' drawled the dark shadow.

'Someone switched off the lights.'

She could hear the hissing sound of exasperation escape his lips. 'It is automated, our contribution to the elimination of light pollution.'

'But you are almost self-sustaining; the hydro and—'

'My, you have been busy educating yourself. Light pollution isn't just about energy; it's about the adverse effects on the natural environment—animals, birds, insects.'

'Oh, well, I wasn't in the dark. I have my phone.'

He gave a disgusted snort. 'You call that a torch?' He waved a high beam light in her face again, and it was an assault on her retinas.

'Stop that!' she squealed, covering her face and turning away. 'Now look what you've made me do,' she added as the contents of her bag spilled out. She dropped down to her knees.

Leo retrieved the paperback that had fallen under some foliage, glanced at the title by torchlight and dropped it into the open bag. 'So you like happy ever afters,' he observed, sounding amused. 'And it's a clever trick, reading in the dark.'

'It wasn't dark when I left the castle,' she retorted.

'I fell asleep in the daytime and when I woke up it was night.' She shrugged and reached out for something to retain her balance as she rose to her feet and realised it was the stone seat of the gazebo erected in his mother's memory. Her eyes flew to his face. 'Oh, you were...' She traced the engraved name with a finger and felt her throat thicken with emotion. 'I disturbed you, I'm sorry,' she said softly.

'Disturbed me?'

His tone sounded strange, and his face, just a blur in the dark, gave no added information.

'Come on, I'll see you back up to your room.'

'Oh, no, I'm fine. I'll...'

'For once in your life, don't argue!'

'All right, all right, there's no need to bellow.'

Above her head he swore, and after a pause she followed the uneven path ahead, which was lit by his powerful torch.

'We were not all Boy Scouts,' she grumbled.

He laughed. 'I wasn't a Boy Scout either. I have never been a team player. Though the local gang took quite a lot of convincing of that fact.'

'Gang?'

'Young men are pack animals, and I wasn't raised in a leafy suburb.'

The matter-of-fact description of his childhood chilled Amy's blood. She had zero idea of what his life had been like in the years before they'd met, and he had rarely mentioned anything beyond the basics. She knew he had lived in several foster homes and had left school with little or no qualifications, which had seemed strange to her at the time, because it was very obvious he was super smart.

They had reached the lawned area.

'I can manage the rest and I'm sorry, I really didn't intend to be out in the dark.'

'I'm going your way.'

'Weren't you going to swim?'

'I might use the pool later, and the next time you feel the need for a midnight skinny-dip you might think of using it yourself.'

Accustomed to the dark now, she could make out the outline of his classical features and it didn't take much imagination to envisage the mocking gleam in his dark eyes as he taunted her.

'I wasn't skinny-dipping; I have a swimsuit on and—' She hesitated.

'What?'

'People might see me in the pool.'

'And that is an issue, why, exactly?'

She hesitated and then admitted, 'Well, there have been a couple of comments, nothing nasty or anything, but staff aren't normally housed where I am and they… we don't have access to the pool and tennis courts or the leisure facilities. I don't want anyone to jump to the wrong conclusions,' she finished, glad the darkness concealed her burning cheeks.

'*The wrong conclusions?*'

Her jaw clamped in response to this display of feigned ignorance. 'You know exactly what I mean.' His torch had been trained into the distance but, as he spoke, he brought it up on her face again like a spotlight. 'And it was only once.'

'Oh, is that why you're so cranky? I've never been anyone's dirty little secret before. Oh, well, a bit of creeping around can be quite stimulating, so I've been told. Or are you talking about a discovery fantasy?'

She batted wildly at his hand, panicked by the insidious tug of desire she felt at his taunts. She heard the sound of the torch hitting something hard a second before they were enclosed in a velvet blackness, as the moon had been swallowed up by a cloud.

The smothering darkness created a dangerous illusion of intimacy and she could feel it like a spider spinning its silken cords around her.

'I don't have anything to keep secret. I know I'm not here long, but it's hard to work as a team if… I just don't want any awkward questions, that's all.'

'Stay still.'

She froze and felt a hand land on her shoulder. 'You were about to step into a pond.'

'How do you know?' she asked, puzzled. She couldn't even see the outline of the castle. She could still feel its presence, though not as intensely as she was aware of Leo's. All her senses were attuned to him.

'I have excellent night vision.'

'Of course you do.'

He laughed at her dry tone. 'That's it,' he added when, encouraged by his guiding hand, she took a step towards him. 'Do you want to have one?'

'Want to have what?'

'Do you want a secret?'

Her throat was dry, her heart beating fast. 'Is that code for something?'

'You know what I'm saying, but I'll spell it out for

you so there is no misunderstanding. Fantasies are not enough. Once is not enough, not nearly enough. I stayed away yesterday because of your migraine but I am asking you now. Amy, do you want to have sex with me?'

'Yes.' She was a mess of screaming hormones, but he didn't have to make beautifully indecent propositions to do that to her. He just had to exist.

He took a deep breath and let it out slowly. His calm was illusionary and it was in danger of shattering at any moment. He was in the grip of a lust that showed no sign of diminishing and the only logical cure was to satiate it.

'You have no idea how glad I am that you said that. We need to finish what we started nearly ten years ago. It doesn't need to be complicated; it's actually very simple.'

She couldn't see his eyes but she was hypnotised—hypnotised by his deep voice, which was like smoke that seemed to wrap around her and vibrate deep inside her like a pulse. The pulse was everywhere, but especially focused between her legs.

'It's not that simple,' she whispered, her protest feeble as she thought, *It's dangerous because I'm falling in love with you again. It's possible I never stopped loving you.*

He leaned in then and she pressed into his hardness as his hands swept down her spine before settling on her bottom, drawing her in even closer.

A sibilant sigh left her lips. 'But you make me ache, Leo.'

'I think we can do something about that ache, don't you?' he rasped against her mouth, and as his tongue flicked along the outline his thumbs were on the corners of her jaw, positioning her lips perfectly for him to plunder.

'I…' The rest of her words were lost inside his mouth as his tongue plunged between her parted lips.

Resistance didn't even cross her mind as she kissed him back with a raw, almost feral desperation, her fingers sliding under his tee-shirt to feel his smooth skin. Revelling in the strength of his hard body and the ridges of muscle that contracted under her touch, she experienced a slug of power as she both heard and felt his groan.

'Is this real?' she wondered, not even realising she had voiced her thoughts out loud until he took her hand and curved it over the rock-hard, pulsing outline in his shorts.

'Does that feel real to you, *cara*?'

'Very, very real…' she mumbled thickly, tightening her grip until he groaned out a protest.

They were stumbling but she didn't know where to until she registered a light… Maybe she was dying and this was the end of a tunnel?

She wasn't dying; it was the swimming pool, with its underwater lighting creating a stunning rippling illuminated effect that was reminiscent of the northern lights.

'I'm never going to make it to a bed,' he bit out.

'Don't apologise,' she mumbled.

Still kissing and half carrying her, he dragged the cushions off one of the recliners on the terrace and threw them on the floor before sinking onto them with her clutched in his arms.

Kneeling face to face, he ripped off his tee-shirt, pulling it over his head in one fluid motion.

She barely registered that the sound that emerged, part gloating greed, part awe, part longing, came from her own lips. Hands resting on his bare shoulders, she kissed her way down his bronzed torso, pulling up only when she reached the waistband of his shorts. Holding his gaze, she slid her hands lower, biting her lip, her eyes fierce with satisfaction when he groaned again.

He jerked her back, his big hands framing her flushed face. 'This isn't going to be *just* sex, *cara*, it's going to be mind-blowing, head-banging sex,' he growled out.

After the *just sex* part, she felt unshed tears press at the back of her eyes. She wanted more than that, but if she told him what she wanted, what she felt about him, it would be a deal-breaker. It was kind of ironic, really. That she had once turned away the man who would now run for the hills at the mention of love or commitment.

She lifted her chin and bit the lobe of his ear and whispered, 'Prove it!'

With bewildering speed, she was flat on her back, the improvised bed of cushions protecting her from the hard surface of the ground.

She felt his body on top of her, but more she felt the staggering power that poured off him, the hunger, the sheer *maleness* that excited her more than she would have thought possible.

He left her alone for a brief moment and peeled off his shorts. The scent of jasmine that spilled from the nearby containers would always, in Amy's head, be associated in future with the sight of him standing there naked and fully aroused, a perfect image of primal male virility.

He was her fantasy in the flesh, made real just for her.

Kneeling, he pulled off her skirt and top and peeled the bikini away from her skin. A moment later she was naked and then he joined her and she was no longer an observer; she was fully involved in this primal mating.

He abruptly interrupted their mutual touching and kissing. 'Protection?' he slurred.

She bit his neck and thought, *Kill me now.*

'You're right, you never were a Boy Scout.'

'I can still make it good for you.'

'I want you inside me!' She nipped his lower lip, drawing a pinprick of blood in her frustration.

'Hang on, let me check…' He rolled over and reached for his shirt and pulled out the wallet he had shoved into his pocket along with his phone.

He emerged triumphant with a silver foil packet.

She smiled and snatched it off him. 'Let me.'

She took her time moving down his body, using his knee as a useful aid to her rising frustration.

His body was slick with salt by the time she took him into her hand. The sinews in his neck distended with the strain he was under as he lifted his head. 'Just do it! I…'

Tipped onto her back, she looked at him, challenge glowing in her eyes as, feet flat on the ground, her knees open in carnal challenge, she waited to be claimed.

It was not a long wait.

A second later, sheathed in her tight slickness, every muscle in his body pumped and primed, he began to move.

Each thrust drove her deeper into herself, and she was aware of him at a cellular level. Each thrust was more pleasure and more torture, the pressure building and building before exploding in a stunning shower of stars.

She floated back to her body slowly, the image of their entwined bodies imprinted behind her closed eyes.

He rolled off her with a grin. 'Witchy woman,' he said, touching the white-blonde streak in the dark of her hair.

'That was…'

'Sex does not have to be complicated.'

'No, it doesn't,' she agreed sadly. *Love* was complicated.

'Shall we take this to a bed? Or do you fancy a swim in the pool?'

'Another time, maybe.'

They ended up in her bed, the transfer taking a little longer because she made him go back and gather their clothes from the poolside, even though they were both more than adequately swathed in towels.

The second time in a bed was gentler, less rushed, more tender, but not any less intense.

Sex for Leo did not usually involve any kind of aftermath; he was an expert at silent dressing in the dark.

So as he lay there in the dark, making sleepy conversation with Amy about modern vinery techniques, which somehow led on to discussing his relationship with his grandfather, he didn't immediately register what was happening.

He was breaking all the rules that he had established over the years for a very good reason—to keep sex a million miles away from an emotional connection.

She sensed his withdrawal and immediately misunderstood the reason for it.

'It's fine, I understand. It's hard; family is so complicated… I wish I had more of a relationship with my mum before she became so ill.'

About to roll away, there was something in her voice that made him lie still. He threw an arm over his head and listened to her soft voice talking in the dark.

'The doctors said I wasn't responsible for the first heart attack. That it was a genetic defect she had been born with.'

He turned on his side to look at her face. 'Why would you feel responsible for her heart attack?'

'I'm not... I wasn't...'

'Amy?'

His tone of voice was uncompromising, and she sighed. It was probably past time to tell him.

'She had her first heart attack when I told them I was leaving to be with you. Dad told me I'd nearly killed her.'

'So this was when you sent me away?' he asked, rigid with tension.

'We had just got back from the hospital. Mum made me promise I would stay. I loved you so much, Leo, but she'd nearly died.'

Hand over his eyes, Leo fell back onto the bed.

He had based everything he'd done over the last nine years on the belief that she had rejected him, that she hadn't truly loved him... But the truth was so much more nuanced than that. Ultimately, his revenge had been to punish her for something that had always been out of her control.

He lay there, stunned, feeling as if a hand had just thrust into his chest and it was squeezing what used to be his heart.

'Why didn't you tell me?' he rasped, seeing her standing there in the doorway that day, the tears gathering in her eyes.

'I... There was no point. It wouldn't have changed anything. And look, it didn't turn out so badly. If I had gone with you, then most likely by now we'd hate one another. Instead, we are having sex, beautiful, fantastic sex.'

'Sex,' he repeated in an odd voice.

'Don't worry, I know you don't want anything else. I know it's just sex and it won't last, but even you have to admit it is totally beautiful.'

She was saying exactly what he wanted to hear, so why did he feel…aggrieved to hear her describing what his perfect relationship would be?

The long pause before he responded made her fear that she had said something wrong, that he had realised the truth—that she still loved him. She had never stopped loving him, but voicing that love would be the end of this and even though they might have no future together, she was going to extract every last scrap of pleasure from the present.

'Yes, totally beautiful.' His voice was husky.

She gave a sigh of relief. It felt as though a barrier between them had fallen, and she felt physically lighter now that she had told him, though of course she hadn't told him all of her secrets.

Her final one was still too painful to share.

CHAPTER TWELVE

AMY WOKE AND turned her head on the pillow, her warm fuzzy feeling dying when she saw the empty space beside her. Leo had been away for two days but was returning today in time for the gala.

As she lay there stretching she saw the scarlet dress hanging behind the door in its transparent cover emblazoned with the designer's name. Her outfit for the gala.

Leo had produced it like a magician before he'd left, expecting her to be pleased. She knew her reaction had disappointed him—she loved it, she really did, and she felt sexy and powerful in it. It wasn't even the fact that she had reservations about being present at the gala. It was more that it was an echo of all times her father had demanded final approval on her mother's outfit for an event.

Her phone rang and she reached for it, grimacing when she saw the caller's identity.

She would ring Ben back. It had only been the previous week when he had rung, asking her if she would consider selling her share in Gourmet Gypsy. The temp, who had worked out really well and had increased their profits, was keen to buy in.

She was torn as the food truck was very much her

baby, though it had only ever been intended to be a temporary stopgap, leading to better things. The better things had not involved staying in a Tuscan castle and becoming the mistress in everything but title to the most gorgeous man in the world.

Leo had already suggested she stay on after the gala, that their arrangement could become open-ended, but she hadn't given him an answer yet. She adored him, she loved him with every cell in her body, but the longer she was here, the harder the inevitable heartbreak would be when it came. And when the man who you loved felt the need to slide the words *just sex* into the conversation every single time you made love, hanging onto any kind of hope was pointless.

She pushed away the decision yet again and instead fingered the red silk of her dress as she walked to the bathroom. Leo would be back later, and for now that was enough.

It was afternoon when the kitchen door opened; it was a quiet moment and she was alone. Amy looked up, emotions she struggled to dampen flaring and dying as the man delivering micro salad from the home farm walked in carrying their order in a cool box.

She was pathetic, she told herself. Even if Leo hadn't been absent for the past two days, she wouldn't have seen anything of him because she was too busy to see him.

Soon she wouldn't see him at all. Even if she took up his offer, there was no promise of permanence, no commitment, but deep down she still had hope and she knew that she wouldn't leave until she lost every scrap of that hope.

She pushed away the thought, which was more than a thought—a reality—but there was no point crying over something that hadn't happened yet. She'd be damned if she was going to waste what time she had with him worrying about the future.

He had texted her when he had arrived back, checking she'd be able to make their meeting. Their so-called *meetings* were often on the beach, sometimes by the pool, when he teased her for having a sentimental attachment to the second place they had made love. *Little did he know!* But mostly these meetings were late at night or early in the morning, before he left her room in cover of darkness.

Several of the staff emerged from the staffroom, where they had been taking a break.

'Have you seen this list, Amy… Chef? We might as well serve this woman fresh air!'

Amy eyed the tablet Jamie was scrolling through. 'Someone with a lot of allergies?' she asked, wondering at the younger woman's annoyed tone. It wasn't as if they weren't all accustomed to accommodating guests' dietary requirements aside of the usual vegetarian and vegan alternatives.

Sensing the unspoken query in Amy's voice, the young chef pushed the tablet along the counter towards her. 'Allergies,' she said as Amy began to read, 'I can do. Food intolerances I can do. Vegan options, well, I'm a vegan. The calorie count that we cannot exceed on each course is also fair enough. But have you seen the dictate on the food groups we're not allowed to combine on a plate? These are not just dietary requirements; it's a straitjacket for any chef! Creativity will go out the—'

While Amy sympathised with the other woman, she adopted a soothing tone. 'Yeah, it doesn't leave much leeway but—'

'But you'd better get used to it, Jamie,' the chef who had been standing at the nearest work station interrupted. 'Because that lady is going to be our new boss.'

'With luck, she won't be spending too much time here,' the younger woman said, displaying crossed fingers before returning to the tablet. 'Do you think they'll be making the announcement tonight?' she wondered gloomily. 'I suppose we could do—'

Her suggestions were a static buzz in Amy's head.

'Our new boss?' she said, aiming for casual and producing strangled.

'You haven't heard?' someone on the other side of the kitchen said in a surprised tone.

'It seems he's serious this time. Apparently, they've been secretly engaged for months. Her name's Sophia.'

'No ring yet, though,' Jamie intervened, typing up notes with a frown. 'And that paper—or rather, scandal sheet—is the rag that wrote that article on the Queen, the old Queen, still being alive. That squid recipe of yours, Amy, do you use…?'

Amy automatically listed the ingredients. 'So Leo is engaged?'

Someone else laughed. 'Do you have *any* footprint on social media?'

'I follow some people.'

'All food-related, right…but there's a whole other world out there.'

'Of bile, gossip and innuendo. Leave her alone.'

* * *

Amy didn't have a clue how she got through the rest of the morning. On autopilot, she delegated the task of co-ordinating the staff who had been brought in for the gala, then waited for the couple of hours that were pencilled in for her time off—supposedly for her *meeting* with Leo.

Her knife skills had raised a few eyebrows as she'd sliced and diced as though her life depended on it. She didn't have a clue who this woman was, but she already hated her. But not as much as she hated Leo and herself, and not necessarily in that order.

He had not promised her anything, but she had *hoped*—she had really hoped—that this had meant more than just sex for him. And all the while he had been planning to make a life with another woman.

She walked through the olive groves that bordered the beach, glad of the shade. When the stony ground gave way to sand, she removed her sandals.

She was early for their assignation, but so was Leo. He was already standing facing the sea when she reached the secluded cove. A voice in her head suggested now was the moment to pause, to get her thoughts in order, but her mortified anger was firmly in charge.

His dark hair was ruffled, his black tee-shirt was tucked into a pair of faded denim cut-offs. Barefoot, Leo was standing on the water's edge, staring out to sea, shading his eyes—perhaps to see the boat with a red sail bobbing on the horizon.

As if sensing her presence, he turned when she was still fifty feet away and watched her approach.

She paused a few feet away from him, the light breeze

whipping her hair into a tangled skein across her face. Even knowing what she now knew—basically, that despite all his simple honesty he was a lying bastard—she had unpinned her hair.

She had worn it loose because he liked it that way and she felt angry with herself for wanting to please him, wanting to hear him say she was beautiful just one last time.

She didn't pause for preliminaries or even notice the smile of welcome on his face morph into an expression of caution.

'Is it true that you are engaged to this Sophia woman?'

For once she had surprised him, but she was too angry to celebrate this triumph over his damned insouciance.

She watched the shock on his face meld into anger. 'How is that relevant?'

Outraged breath hissed through her flared nostrils as she pulled herself up to her full and unimpressive five foot three. 'You can ask that?'

'I just did,' he pointed out mildly.

She scowled furiously. 'I don't sleep with married men.'

'I'm not married.'

She threw him a narrow-eyed challenge and gritted out, 'But you're engaged?'

Now the question was out, there was no going back, no pretending, and she felt an icy fist of dread tighten in her belly. Because, beneath her aggressive façade, Amy was willing him to deny it, or laugh at the suggestion.

He didn't, and she died a little bit inside.

'Can I ask where you got this inside information?'

He had the utter, unbelievable cheek to act offended. 'Everyone knows, apparently.'

Except me.

Humiliation tasted bitter in her mouth.

'The entire kitchen is talking about it, about *her...*' The venom in her own voice shocked her, as taunting images of the gala's guest of honour, the subject of Amy's recent furtive internet searches, flashed before her eyes.

The blonde with the trashy reality television credentials was a perfect match for the Romano heir. The men her name had been linked with were all rich and famous, and none of them said a bad word about her. She had been equally discreet.

The perfect partner for Leo.

'You're jealous.'

She clenched her fists and tossed her head as she glared up at him. 'Grow up, Leo. I don't care who you marry! You can have a harem for all I care, but I do object to not being given the information to make an informed choice. You obviously don't give a damn when it comes to cheating but, call me old-fashioned,' she hissed, 'I bloody do, you bastard!'

She finished her diatribe on a breathless gasp, doubled over at the waist.

'I thought you had more sense than to listen to gossip.'

Her head came up with a jerk. 'Don't you dare patronise me, Leo!'

He stepped forward, clasping both her wrists, and pulled her upright.

'You are aware that I am supposedly being married off to at least three women a month?'

'Your modesty is one of your most charming characteristics.'

There was zero warning as he reached down and ran his hand over the brand-new silk kimono she wore over a strapless bikini. 'That's new—I like it, but I prefer you without it.'

The sound of her hand connecting with his cheek was shocking.

'Oh, God, I am so, so sorry! I shouldn't have… You just make me so mad! How the hell did you think it was appropriate to make a pass at me at this moment? I've never hit anyone in my entire life. I am mortified…'

He caught the shaking hand she had pressed to her mouth and pulled it to his lips, holding her eyes as he spread her fingers and kissed her palm. 'I'm sorry I wound you up, *cara*. I admit I was a bit of a bastard.'

Amy blinked at the unexpected climbdown, shock combining with confusion, hot tingles spreading like a web from her palm along her nerve-endings.

'I really shouldn't have done that, though.'

'Your vicious little tongue does a lot more harm than your left hook, *cara*. You barely touched me.' The levity in his words were not reflected in the tension-carved angles and planes of his face, which projected an intense, driven quality.

'I should be immune to gossip. I *am* immune.' Or he'd thought he was. 'I usually ignore it when people write lies about me, when I find human rats going through my recycling bin looking for private information. It doesn't matter to me what strangers think.'

It mattered what Amy thought of him, though.

The discovery of this vulnerability had not made him

overly sympathetic to her distress and he'd deliberately goaded her until she'd snapped.

Her eyes flickered down to their single point of contact, which still hadn't been broken. He hadn't let go of her hand and there was something hypnotic about the way his thumb was tracing tiny arabesques on her palm.

When she drew her hand back and nursed it against her chest, he made no attempt to prevent her. 'I am not a stranger,' she said huskily.

'No, you're not, and I shouldn't have reacted like that. I am not engaged—not to Sophia nor to anyone else. Despite my grandfather's constant matchmaking, I remain single. Do you believe me?' His ink-dark eyes scanned her face.

The reply came without a pause. 'Yes, I do...' In her head she could hear herself saying those words standing in a church but, before her fantasy could solidify, she pushed it away. 'Believe you, that is,' she tacked on, hastily adding, 'I suppose it's only natural that your grandfather wants an heir.'

He might be holding out but one day, perhaps when his grandfather realised that Leo did not react well to being pushed, he would oblige, and produce the future Romano generation.

An image of dark-eyed children arranged by height flashed before her eyes. Children they might have had together in another life.

'I know what we are...or rather what we are not. What we share is just sex. I get that.' She should do; he'd said it often enough. *As if she was likely to forget when he recited it like a post-coital mantra.*

'But honesty is important to me and there are some

lines that I am not willing to cross.' Lines, she realised, that could look very blurred just because she burned so fiercely for this man.

But if she bent her own rules and crossed those lines once, she would never stop crossing them, and she would end up a paler version of the person she was.

Someone she didn't like.

She jerked as a wave lapped over her toes with a hiss and retreated.

'Sophia is coming to the gala,' he said.

Her toes dug into the wet sand. 'I know this, and me being here is still an exercise in humiliation.' Her throat closed up as she angrily blinked away tears. 'Was she supposed to be part of it? I just didn't realise how far you would take it… I feel pretty stupid right now.'

'You feel stupid? How the hell do you think I feel?'

Unnerved by the raw anger in his voice, she took a step back.

'Do you think any of this is going the way I planned? Nine years ago, I felt happier than I'd ever been, ever dreamt I could be, and then you walked away from me. Well, maybe it was all for the good. Before my grand-father found me, I had already discovered I had skills, a knack for making money. Initially, it was just about try-ing to prove myself to you and your family, then I dis-covered I was really good at thinking outside the box.'

'And making even more money.'

He nodded and gave a negligent shrug. 'Yes. Seeing you reminds me of what I once thought my life was. It re-minds me of all my weaknesses.' His heavy lids drooped.

'You think I'm a weakness?'

Amy was half fascinated and half repelled by his admission.

'I think you are my nemesis.' He paused, his chest lifting as he sucked in a deep breath. 'You have a face and a body that would tempt a saint and I am definitely no saint.' He gave a devil-on-steroids white grin and caught her by the waist and…did he drag her towards him, or did she throw herself at him?

Amy wasn't sure. It was one of those moments when the cord that seemed to connect them was almost visible as she strained to press closer to him.

'It doesn't matter what I say, my body betrays me…' The groan that followed his laugh had a tortured sound that she physically felt. 'As does yours,' he said, his mouth moving down the column of her throat. 'I can smell it on you. You're ready for me now.'

She whimpered and his dark eyes flared before his mouth covered hers in a devouring kiss.

Their mutual frantic kissing took them several feet from the water's edge, where they collapsed to their knees onto the sand, pulling off each other's clothes, hands on hot skin as they fell onto the sand.

'Sorry, I'm squashing you.'

'No!' She placed one hand on the back of his head and held him where he was. 'I like it.'

'This is…' he started to say.

Just sex.

'What's wrong?' he asked sharply.

She shook her head, an intent expression settling on her face as she traced the sharp angles of his face with the forefinger of her free hand. Then she arched her back to increase the delicious friction of their bodies.

His eyes were black as he turned his head, taking her palm and kissing it before catching her probing finger and drawing it into his mouth and sucking. His hands moved up and down her body before he lowered his head and kissed her, sliding his tongue between her parted lips.

This was no practised technique; it was all fire and raw need, and Amy felt as though she was burning up from the inside.

'Open your legs for me,' he urged throatily.

A hungry sound, half growl, half moan of longing, left her lips as he thrust into her willing heat. Her breath left her in one long sibilant hiss as her body stretched to accommodate him and hold him tight, her head flung back in sheer pleasure.

She could feel him plunging deep inside her, hot and hard, every cell aware of him. She moved as one with him, swiftly climbing to the peak with him and then leaping off the top with such a tumultuous freefall of sensation that she didn't know where he began and she ended.

They lay sprawled on the sand, both breathing hard.

'Don't move,' she begged when he began to roll off her.

He lifted his head and kissed her flushed cheek. 'I have to—there are drinks before the party with a select few guests and my grandfather has arrived.'

He stood up in one fluid motion. She sighed dreamily. His body was a work of art, utterly perfect in every way.

'And I suppose I should go back to work,' she said, not moving.

He was fastening the clip on the waist of his shorts when he paused.

'What is it?' she asked, sensing his unease.

He paused but didn't meet her eyes as he said, 'I'm sorry if I hurt you.'

She suddenly just wanted to hug him—not in a sexual way but to provide comfort. 'I'm really not so fragile.'

He gave a half nod and felt a rush of relief. Lust had never taken him over so totally before and the idea of hurting her was more painful than a knife blade.

'You didn't hurt me, but maybe I hurt you?' She rose from the sand and stood behind him, running her finger along the small, raised crescents on the satiny skin of his muscled back, from her fingernails clutching him in sheer ecstasy. 'I don't think I broke the skin, though.'

'My little cat.' He turned and caught her in his arms and kissed her, hard and hungry.

'You're the one purring,' she retorted, wading through the sand to where her bikini top had landed. 'Where are my…? Thanks,' she said as he handed her the bottom half of her bikini.

He watched her slide the bottoms over her slim, shapely thighs while he struggled with what to say. He never usually shared, he never explained, but it was a concession of sorts. 'Just to warn you, Sophia will also be at the pre-party drinks.'

Amy felt a pressure in her chest as she adjusted the string ties of her bikini bottoms.

The long beat of silence lengthened.

'Listen, Amy, I…'

'Is this some sort of test?' She rounded on him.

'No, of course not.'

'Then why did you tell me that?' And spoil a perfect moment.

'*Dio*, but I can't win with you, can I? You wanted me to *share*.'

'You call that sharing?' She hooted. 'Rubbing in the fact that you'll be upstairs with *Sophia* while I'm cooking her dinner in the kitchen.' She managed a shrug. 'Well, the joke's on you. The kitchen is actually where I prefer to be.'

'Yes, I know you are queen there. As for Sophia, our paths may have crossed, but we have never been lovers. I'm not her type.'

Her eyes widened fractionally. 'So she is—'

'In love with someone else who… Well, it's not my story to tell, but I can tell you that she wants to make this someone—'

'Jealous?'

He shook his head. 'More like make them realise that she will not wait around for them forever. This is only an assumption on my part, you understand. I'm not getting involved. I just agreed to say nothing, and it gets my grandfather off my back for a few days.'

Not getting involved… So, nothing new there, she thought, pushing down her resentment.

'You're not going to tell me any more than that, are you?'

'No,' he agreed with an enigmatic smile.

'Did anyone ever tell you that you have a terrible attitude?' Amy broke off, gasping as a wave washed over her feet, swirling around her calves until it retreated with a soft hiss. A second wave peaked as it approached.

Leo caught her hand and pulled her back onto the dry sand. The impetus brought their bodies onto a collision course.

The air left Amy's body with a soft oomph as she stepped back. She went to take another step back but his hands came to rest on her bottom, and the impulse to pull free vanished in a puff of smoke.

She tilted her head back and looked into his face. He brushed the hair from her cheek and hooked a finger under her chin, bringing her face up to his. The featherlight touch made her think of his hands on her body, his fingers inside her body, and the things he did with his tongue.

She cursed her imagination, and her breathing had slowed to almost nothing as his nose grazed hers. His breath was warm on her cheek as his mouth moved soft as a whisper over her lips.

'While it lasts, we are exclusive.'

She blanked the *while it lasts* and focused on the *exclusive* part as she nodded in agreement.

'You don't leave me much energy for anyone else, anyway,' he murmured against her mouth before his tongue sank hungrily into the sweet welcoming depths.

She kissed him back, her hands winding into the dark hair at the nape of his neck. 'It's been a bad morning, and everyone is a bit tense about tonight, especially with the entire gala hysteria.'

'You love a challenge,' he said with a heartless lack of sympathy as he lifted her into his arms so she could wind her legs around his waist and began to deliver a series of slow open-mouthed kisses down her throat. 'I'm looking forward to seeing you in that dress. Next year you'll be…'

His words cleared the sensual fog that suffused her and she became achingly aware of the carnal pressure of his erection against her core and the fact she was grinding against it to increase that delicious pressure.

Hands on his chest, she shimmed down until she was standing in front of him, her chest heaving.

'Next year? I won't be here next year. I was only meant to be here for six weeks.'

The truth was she had been drifting, avoiding the good offer from Ben's friend, partly because she didn't want to think ahead. She wanted to enjoy every moment.

'Who knows where any of us will be next year, so live in the moment.' His voice had a hardness to it, but not as hard as his stare, which was skewering her. 'Don't act like I'm holding you here against your will.'

He didn't need to, and he knew it. She wore the dresses he wanted her to, she went to parties she didn't want to go to…and suddenly her resentment rose.

'I couldn't walk out before the gala, that wouldn't be fair.'

'That is so bloody kind of you.'

Her jaw tightened at his sarcasm.

'We're having fun. Why are you so afraid to admit it?' he asked.

'I know it's just convenient for you, having me around when you're here.'

A raw laugh erupted from his chest as, hands in his hair, he turned back to the sea before, moments later, swinging back to face her. 'Convenient! You are many things, Amy, but *convenient* is not one of them.'

'You're never going to forgive me for the past, are you?'

A hissing sound of exasperation left his lips. 'Let it go, Amy. I appreciate that the situation with your mother was horrendous and you felt obliged to stay, but you could have contacted me, explained.'

She could tell by the way it exploded out of him that this had been eating away at him.

'I did try to contact you.'

'Just leave it, Amy.'

'You don't believe me! I did ring you, but you'd already blocked me and then it was number unknown. I even tried to follow you on social media, I was so desperate. But then...'

'Fine, you tried, I believe you, but just let it lie now, Amy.'

His attitude, as if he was doing her a massive favour, snapped something inside her.

'I got on a train, even though I didn't know where I was going, just because I needed to tell you something important.'

'What,' he mocked, 'that love conquers all?'

'No, that I was pregnant.'

In the aftershock of her explosive reveal there was a pulsating silence that seemed to go on for ever.

'You were pregnant and you didn't tell me?'

She couldn't take her eyes off the pulse throbbing in his cheek.

'I just told you I tried to call you.'

'My baby?' He turned to look at her, his dark eyes bleak and filled with nothing resembling love or even liking. 'Where is he now?'

'I had a miscarriage.'

'And you could have told me that how many times over the past weeks?'

'What would have been the point? It's history.'

'Is it? Or is it your version of history? How do I know there was ever a baby? How do I know you didn't get rid of him or have him adopted? I could have a child out there...'

She listened to his increasingly irrational flow of accusations, growing colder and colder inside.

'If any of that is what you truly think me capable of, I think you should start advertising for a new chef and do not expect me to work my notice. Also, this Cinderella doesn't wear ballgowns and I hate red!' she shrieked.

CHAPTER THIRTEEN

THE THING AMY had always feared had happened. She'd always been secretly afraid that if he had known about the baby he would have rejected her and now, nine years later, that was exactly what he had done! There were no tears, though, not even when her hot emotions cooled to cold misery as she jogged back to the castle, not looking back. She slowed to a more sedate pace as she went past the musicians who were setting up in the marquee and the lighting technicians who were putting the last touches to the laser display that was timed for midnight, and went straight to her room.

She would leave tomorrow, she decided, looking at her dry-eyed reflection in the mirror, but she couldn't leave them in the lurch tonight. Ben could have the business; she wanted a total change.

The annoying stitch in her side took a long time to go away and by the time it had subsided there wasn't really time for a shower. But she made time before dressing for work, glancing at the dress still hanging up. She shook her head and straightened her shoulders before she donned her kitchen whites.

She walked into the kitchen and realised how much she would miss this place.

But not him—she hated him. He had made her love him all over again and she would never forgive him for what he'd said to her. Those accusations, they were… She shuddered when she thought of his words, remembering the emptiness in her life after she'd lost the baby.

Leo didn't watch her leave. He turned in the opposite direction and stood there, staring out at the sea, his thoughts churning.

He *had* blocked her calls, he remembered now, taking petty satisfaction from the action, or maybe he had just been protecting himself from the fact that he didn't think she'd try to contact him.

The idea of her being alone, like his own mother, coping with the tragedy of loss with no support, crushed something inside him. Maybe he should be asking himself why she hadn't trusted him enough to tell him about the baby when she'd finally opened up about her mother.

And when she had told him about the baby, what had he done? He'd blown any chance of them being together, of having a family together. A look of shock flickered across his face as he turned his back on the ocean. He *wanted* a family. He wanted a family with Amy. He loved her to distraction—he always had and he always would—but he'd been too much of a coward to admit it to himself, let alone to tell her. He'd been emotionally cut off and she had…she had given everything and asked nothing from him in return.

He walked back across the beach, realising that he was in danger of becoming just like his grandfather, alienating everyone he loved.

* * *

'What time are you heading off to mingle, Chef?' Jamie teased when the party was in full swing and they were enjoying a lull.

'I'm going to give it a miss.'

'No, you have to go, to represent us.'

Jamie's voice died at a nudge from someone.

'You not feeling too good, Amy?'

'Not really,' Amy admitted. 'But I'll be fine,' she said, producing a grin that didn't fool anyone.

'Why don't you head off, have an early night?'

Like a drowning man, she clutched at the suggestion even though she wasn't sure where it came from. 'I think I might. I'll just… Oh, dear!'

She could hear voices, see faces, but then she swayed and only saw black dots dancing before her eyes.

'Leo!' she cried before the blackness encompassed her.

It was a graceful faint and, luckily for her, a good catch.

'Jamie, find a doctor!' one of the other chefs ordered.

She came to and groggily tried to lift her head. 'I need to…'

'You need to lie down.'

'I am,' she said, her hands warm against the stone of the floor she was lying on. 'I should get up.' Then she felt pain and realised she couldn't.

His grandfather looked at the glass in Leo's hand and raised a brow.

'That isn't your first drink tonight.'

Leo flashed a sardonic smile at his grandfather. 'And

it probably won't be my last, but don't worry, I won't disgrace the family name.'

'So where is our chef?'

'I don't think she'll be coming. In fact, I'm pretty sure I'm going to need a new chef.' He waited but there was no reply.

'What, no lecture on the reckless disregard for social structure or even the dangers of sleeping with the help?' he mocked, sliding deeper into his chair.

The old man's expression didn't change, despite the languid pose and the provocative attitude of his heir. 'So, I take it you're just going to sit there feeling sorry for yourself all night.'

Leo surged to his feet. The action and his fierce masculinity combined with the air of danger he was projecting, drawing stares.

'You're an idiot, this I already knew, but I had no idea until this moment that you were also a coward, Leo. I am ashamed.'

His eyes flashing fire, Leo towered over the older man, but he only held the pose for a split second before his shoulders drooped.

'So am I,' he said with a lopsided smile before he drained his champagne glass. Guilt had made him lash out at her—the knowledge that she had needed him and he hadn't been there for her.

It was fear that had stopped him from following her, from begging for her forgiveness. Fear that she would reject him for the last time, and he wouldn't blame her if she did.

'I can change.'

'Don't tell me—tell her.'

A suited figure appeared, sensing the atmosphere but squaring his shoulders anyway, and interrupted two generations of Romanos. 'I'm sorry, but I thought you should know that…'

A prickle of icy premonition ran down Leo's spine. 'What, man?'

'Miss Sinclair is unwell. She just collapsed.'

'Where is she?'

'She's still in the kitchen. We thought it best not to move her until a doctor had seen her.'

Leo flashed a frantic look at his grandfather, who just said, 'Go!'

He looked at the messenger as Leo vanished and said drily, 'Like I, or anyone else, could stop him.'

The kitchen had been cleared of staff, so the only people present were the young female chef and a doctor who was here as a guest, not professionally.

The icy hand of dread in his chest tightened. The guilt clawed at him like a fist as he thought of the last words he had said to her. He'd found her again after nine long years; she was his heart and his home, and now he could have lost her.

She was young; she couldn't die.

But his mother had been young and she had died.

He closed off the internal dialogue, his attempt to run to her side foiled by the doctor.

'A word first, please.'

Leo flashed a look at the pale, immobile figure on the floor. She looked so small, so fragile, so broken.

Swallowing his impatience, he allowed the doctor to take him a little to one side. 'What's happened?'

'I assume I'm speaking to you as her partner and not her employer?'

It didn't even occur to Leo to deny it and he gave a tight nod. 'Yes.'

'Well, it will be for the hospital to confirm but it appears that she could possibly be miscarrying.'

'What? She can't be... You're saying she's *pregnant? Now?*'

The doctor raised his bushy brows. 'Yes. Miss Sinclair didn't realise it either but, from our conversation, I would suggest it's still very early. It's not unusual at this stage but, given her history...'

'But that was nine years ago...and yes,' he added fiercely. 'That was mine too. Is she in danger?'

'I'll be much happier if she's in hospital.'

The blood drained from Leo's face. 'The baby?'

'I'm afraid I couldn't get a heartbeat, but that's not diagnostic; the hospital has much better equipment than my stethoscope. The air ambulance should be here directly.'

Leo usually prided himself on being the master of his emotions, but appearing supportive and not scared out of his mind was one of the hardest things he had ever done.

He took a deep breath and squatted down beside the prone figure who was covered in about ten coats. He glanced at the young girl beside Amy and nodded his thanks.

She smiled back. 'Chef, shall I...?'

'You go—and thanks, Jamie.'

After Jamie left, Leo took Amy's hand.

'You're missing your party. No, you can't shout at me,' she added when he looked ready to explode. 'I'm the walking wounded... Well, there's not much walking.'

'Are you in pain?'

'No, I'm fine.'

'You're a terrible liar,' he said, gently pushing a strand of hair from her cheek.

She didn't respond but she didn't agree either. She was a good liar—she had been lying to herself for so long that she had, until recently, actually believed the lies she'd told herself. The *I am over Leo* lie, the *I don't love Leo any more* lie.

Knowing she was carrying his baby and that it was likely she would lose it had ripped the plaster off those particular lies in the most painful way possible.

'I'm sorry about this. I know we were usually careful about protection, and that this is the last thing—'

He pressed a finger to her lips. 'Hush now and don't tell me what I want or feel.'

'Oh!' she fretted. 'You're being so kind to me. Jamie won't tell anyone about us, I asked her not to. And I think maybe I said stuff about you to the doctor too, because I panicked a bit.'

He swore the air blue and cradled her face gently between his big hands. 'You know I'm never kind and Jamie can shout it from the rooftops if she wants to, for all I care.' If he wasn't so engaged with the immediate priority he would have been doing some shouting himself.

He kissed her forehead with a tender reverence that brought tears to her eyes because she knew he was only doing it because of the baby.

He turned at the rustle of activity around the doorway. 'The ambulance is here.'

She closed her eyes. 'I hate hospitals.'

'Everyone hates hospitals.'

Her gaze was fluttering around the room in panic. 'Mum was in and out so many times, and there were so many deathbed scenes before the real one. She liked me to read to her and—'

'Don't worry, I will be with you.'

Her brown eyes focused on his face. 'Promise?'

He caught her hand and didn't let go. 'I promise.'

Amy didn't remember much about the helicopter flight to the hospital, she just remembered clinging to Leo's hand as though it were her lifeline.

It was a blur of white ceilings and test after test, but the only one that mattered to her was the ultrasound. The moment when they heard the heartbeat.

'Do you want to see the baby?' the doctor asked with a smile.

Leo's grip turned her fingers white and when she turned to look at him, tears streaming down her cheeks, his were wet too.

'Mr Romano, I can talk to your partner or—'

'Together.' He flashed a look at Amy, who nodded her approval. 'We will face this together, Doctor.'

'As you now know, the baby is well, but there are issues.'

'Is it like last time?' Amy asked, her voice shaking. 'I have to know.'

'From what you've told me, that is a possibility.'

'There was a lot of blood. Are you sure the baby is fine?'

'A little can look like a lot, Miss Sinclair.'

'Please call me Amy.'

'Well, Amy, you have what we call a placenta praevia,

which means the placenta has developed low down in the uterus. Sometimes, it can completely block the cervix, but in your case there is a partial blockage. The bleeding you experienced was from a tear in a blood vessel.'

'That doesn't sound good,' Amy said in a shaky voice.

'Cases of placenta praevia can, and do, resolve themselves as the pregnancy progresses, in which case normal birth is possible. Otherwise, a C-section is advised.'

'So that's the positive stuff; what about the scary stuff?'

Leo did not often feel humble, but he did now as he watched Amy face this situation head-on, even though he could feel she was shaking with terror.

She was the strongest person he knew, he thought as possessive pride surged through his body.

'Well, premature labour is a possibility, especially at this very early stage, and a rupture of a major blood vessel is a danger for mother and baby. However,' he added quickly to forestall Leo's interruption, 'that is the worst-case scenario. Further pregnancies would need to be carefully monitored.'

'There is a risk to Amy?' Leo asked hoarsely.

'Future pregnancies could be perfectly normal,' the doctor said, with what seemed like unnatural cheer to Leo.

Leo set his jaw firmly. There would not be any more pregnancies. Amy was his family; she was all he needed. Losing her wasn't a risk worth taking. Would Amy be OK with adoption?

'Many cases resolve themselves at this stage. Most don't even require bed rest, just not activity that puts strain on the pelvis. However, in your case, as there's

still a small amount of bleeding, I personally would pre-
scribe bed rest.'

'That means I have to stay in hospital?' she faltered,
the idea filling her with horror. But she lifted her chin
and squared her shoulders; she would do anything to
save this baby.

'Actually, when circumstances allow, we are quite
happy for the situation to be managed at home, monitored, obviously...'

'Yes,' Leo said immediately, then turned to Amy, who
gave a small nod of tentative relief.

'I'll leave you to discuss things in private. If you have
any questions, I will be available.'

Amy waited until the door closed and they were alone.
The room contained one less person but now they were
alone it somehow felt smaller, or maybe Leo felt bigger.
Ignoring the urge to clutch his hand, she unwrapped her
fingers from his and pulled her hand away.

She sighed. 'You're being supportive, incredibly supportive, and I appreciate that, I really do.' Because of
the sort of man he was, he'd put his own feelings on the
back-burner.

'I know you won't believe me, but I really didn't know
about the baby.'

'I do believe you,' he shot back.

'Oh...w...well, that's good,' Amy stuttered out, thrown
by his swift, unequivocal response. 'I'm still in shock,'
she admitted. 'I mean, I think it must have been that first
time. I mean, we were in such a rush...'

'I can identify with shock.'

'Look, I can see you were in an awkward position

there with the consultant, but I understand that you don't want your life disrupted to this extent. I'll be fine in hospital.'

He pressed his hands palm down on the bed and leaned in towards her, capturing her tear-filled eyes with his dark, intent stare.

'Well, I *won't* be fine with you staying in hospital. In fact, the only way you're staying here would be if I moved in with you.'

'But...'

He placed a finger to her lips and looked at her from under the sweep of his crazily long, dark eyelashes. 'You are carrying my child, Amy. I wasn't there for you last time and I will never, ever forgive myself for that, but this time I'm fully on board. I owe you an apology for the way I reacted when you told me about the first pregnancy. I didn't mean any of it, but it was still unforgivable.'

Her heart fluttered in her chest as she studied his face and saw total sincerity.

'You have forgiven me for not telling you?'

'There's nothing to forgive you for, but I'm not sure I've forgiven myself for being so judgemental.' His lips curled in a grimace of self-disgust. 'It was my guilt talking and I took it out on your. It seems that being in love does not make me any less a coward or a bastard.'

'In *love*?'

'I never stopped loving you, Amy. I understand now that when you pushed me away you were in an impossible position, all alone. And my response was to block your calls. I'm disgusted with myself.' The ring of truth in his voice made her eyes fill. 'You are brave and strong and never let me get away with a thing. I have been lying to myself about my feelings for you for the past nine years, because I couldn't own the pain, the hurt. I never stopped hurting after I lost you.'

She sniffled and he brushed a tear from her cheek. 'Please tell me that this means you're happy?'

'I am, of course I am, but this can't work,' she said sadly. 'If I lose this baby,' she said, pressing her hands protectively over her belly. 'And it could happen—'

'If it does, there will be no more babies. You will not risk yourself. I will not permit it. If I lost you, I would never recover! And I never want to relive that moment when I saw you lying on the floor.' He shuddered.

'But your grandfather wants an heir. I don't want to come between you and him.'

'He has me,' Leo declared, looking and sounding every inch the Italian autocrat. 'If that is not enough for him, he can reproduce himself! The only thing that matters to me is being enough for you, *cara*.'

Tears spilling down her face, she nodded and held out her arms. 'You are very much enough for me, Leo.' A flicker of a smile curved her lips upwards. 'In fact, there are times when you are too much for me.'

He kissed her as though she were made of precious glass, gentle but with the sort of tender emotion that made fresh tears spring to her eyes.

'None of this seems real,' she said, taking his big hands between her smaller ones. 'This is so crazy—I'm lying in a hospital bed, terrified more than I can explain, and yet I'm also insanely happy because I love you, Leo. I don't have the words to tell you just how much.'

'We will get through this together, my love, and you never need be afraid again, or alone.'

EPILOGUE

LEO, WHO HAD been walking up and down the library with the pushchair, stopped when Amy appeared in a rustle of silk with the photographer in tow. He stopped dead, a look of awe spreading across his face.

'Leo!' She performed a graceful twirl.

'You look beautiful…' He took a deep breath and stepped back, bowing at the waist in homage to the figure in ivory silk.

'Isn't it bad luck for you to see me in the dress before the wedding? Actually, you don't look bad yourself.' That had to be the understatement of the century.

'That dress has been hanging in our bedroom for the past two weeks.'

'Good point,' she conceded, her nose wrinkling critically as she squinted at her reflection in the full-length mirror. 'You don't think it's a bit too tight still up top?' she queried, pressing her hands to her chest. 'I know it's already been let out, but the feeding is making me a bit…'

She tiptoed across to the pushchair. 'Is she asleep?'

'See for yourself.'

A big pair of golden-brown eyes looked up at her. 'You know she's bound to bawl during the service, but then I suppose without her we might not be getting married.'

Leo frowned. 'Are you suggesting I only proposed to you because of our spectacularly beautiful daughter, our miracle baby?'

'Of course not!'

'Or that you said yes because of her?'

'No, I said yes because...' She gave a contented sigh and rubbed her hand lovingly across his lean cheek. 'I love you, Leo,' she said huskily. 'This...us, everything... it all seems like a lovely dream sometimes.'

Leo glanced across at the photographer, who was scrolling through the photos on his camera, oblivious to their conversation.

'And to answer your question, it is perfect *up top,* as you so quaintly phrase it, and in every other place too, as are you, *cara.'*

As Leo leant in and whispered in her ear she flushed and angled a warning glance in the direction of the photographer, who was still engrossed in what he was doing.

Leo rolled his eyes and muttered, 'He's in a world of his own.' before raising his voice. 'So how did it go? Lawrence?'

The photographer looked up with a vague expression. 'Sorry?'

'How did the shoot go? Is it in the bag now?'

'It looks great to me.'

'It looked great to you the last time too, but my wife—who I'm pretty sure is your worst nightmare client—had other ideas.'

'Oh, no, she isn't, not at all. She's just a perfectionist.'

'Ignore him, Lawrence,' Amy interrupted, throwing her husband a killer look. 'I just wanted it to be right, and it's perfect now.'

'I'll send you the proofs for a final review,' the photographer promised her.

Amy turned to face her husband as the other man left. 'Now you have my full attention.'

'You know you take multitasking to a crazy level. A wedding, a christening and a photoshoot.'

She grinned. 'Sorry, I had no idea he was going to roll up this morning. We had arranged it for next week, but he got his calendar confused.'

'Will I pass?'

'You have baby sick on your shoulder.'

'Oh, God!' he groaned, turning to try and see his shoulder. 'Will anyone notice?'

'I can smell it.'

'Well, you have cream on your behind.'

'I do not!' she said, trying to resist the temptation to look and failing. 'Oh, no! I knew I should have waited to change until *after* the shoot.'

'I can smell you as well, and you smell delicious. In fact, you make me hungry.' She fell into his arms with a sigh as he framed her face, his long, tanned fingers pushing into her hair. 'I love your witchy streak.'

'Leo, I knew it was a bad idea to have this photoshoot today. I mean, who in their right mind writes a cookery book when they're pregnant?'

He nuzzled her neck, the tiny moist bites sending sensual shudders throughout her body. Fighting the urge to relax into his embrace, which the small sane portion of her brain told her would be fatal, she pressed her hands to his shoulders, but the sinewy strength felt so good she ended up holding on, not pushing him away.

'You do.'

Amy blinked. She had forgotten the question as her finger trailed down his freshly shaven cheek.

'Admit it, you would have gone totally crazy on bed rest for all those months with no distractions.'

She laughed and returned his kiss with enthusiasm. 'It's true, I would have.'

It hadn't just been the inactivity; it had been the constant fear of losing the baby. She had been utterly dismissive when Leo had first pitched the idea that she write a cookery book but, once she had begun, it had been a sanity-saver—a marvellous distraction. She had never expected that it would be published, that had been a bonus, and she was still nervous about the outcome.

But today wasn't about the book, or the mouthwatering photos that seemed to now be in the bag, it was about the commitment they were about to make in front of, if not the world, the people that mattered in their lives, plus her father, who, despite everything he'd done, still mattered to her.

Amy was just grateful that Leo hadn't vetoed his invitation and understood she needed him there, even though the two men were never going to be friends. In fact, Leo loved her so much that he'd also helped extricate her father—and Gourmet Gypsy—from all involvement with his former 'friends' from prison. Now, George Sinclair was living a legitimate, albeit very quiet, life in forced retirement.

A cry made them both turn to the pushchair, where plump legs were kicking.

'But oh…it was worth it, wasn't it, Leo?'

Leo's eyes went to the small bundle with a mop of dark hair. 'Worth it? My God…she is just so perfect—'

His fervent agreement morphed into a laugh when the perfect dark-haired bundle in the pushchair started to wail. 'That child has a real set of lungs on her.'

She saw the expression in his eyes as he looked at their daughter and felt a burning ache of love in her chest.

'She needs changing—'

'No, let me,' he said, leaning past her. 'Your dress.'

'I thought it was already ruined.'

The baby on his shoulder calmed as he patted her back. 'I was joking—you look perfect. You always look perfect.'

She laughed. 'Now I know you're lying.'

His expression grew solemn. 'You, my love, my life, are my truth.'

* * * * *

If you were captivated by
Reclaimed on Romano's Terms*, then be sure to check out these other steamy stories from Kim Lawrence!*

Her Forbidden Awakening in Greece
Awakened in Her Enemy's Palazzo
His Wedding Day Revenge
Engaged in Deception
Last-Minute Vows

Available now!

Get up to 4 Free Books!

We'll send you 2 free books from each series you try PLUS a free Mystery Gift.

FREE
Value Over
$25

Both the **Harlequin Presents** and **Harlequin Medical Romance** series feature exciting stories of passion and drama.